PUFFIN CLASSICS
Timeless Tales from Marwar

ADVANCE PRAISE FOR THE BOOK

'Stories which travelled centuries to come to you—please read them
soon—because they still have centuries to travel. These folk tales from
Rajasthan slither like serpents in the mind of the reader and tickle the
imagination'—Gulzar

Timeless Tales
from Marwar

VIJAYDAN DETHA

TRANSLATED FROM THE RAJASTHANI BY VISHES KOTHARI

Introduction by ARUNA ROY

PUFFIN BOOKS

An imprint of Penguin Random House

PUFFIN BOOKS

USA | Canada | UK | Ireland | Australia
New Zealand | India | South Africa | China | Singapore

Puffin Books is part of the Penguin Random House group of companies whose
addresses can be found at global.penguinrandomhouse.com

Published by Penguin Random House India Pvt. Ltd
4th Floor, Capital Tower 1, MG Road,
Gurugram 122 002, Haryana, India

First published in Puffin Books by Penguin Random House India 2020

Text copyright © The legal heirs of Vijaydan Detha 2020
Translation copyright © Vishes Kothari 2020

ISBN 9780143448280

Typeset in Minion Pro by Manipal Technologies Limited, Manipal

Printed at Repro India Limited

www.penguin.co.in

This is a legitimate digitally printed version of the book and therefore might not
have certain extra finishing on the cover.

To
Dadosa and Dadisa,
Nanosa and Nanima,
Bada Nanosa and Nanisa,
because of whom I felt these stories are mine

With special thanks to Mahendra Dan Detha for rights and
permissions, and for his support

Contents

Introduction

I want to share with all of you my joy of discovering Vijaydan Detha's collection of Rajasthani folk tales, the classic *Batan ri Phulwari*, produced as retellings in *Timeless Tales from Marwar*. Fondly known as Bijji, he introduced himself as a writer of stories. Behind those simple words lay a treasure trove of tales told in a unique and inimitable style. He was a chronicler of Rajasthani culture through its abundant and rich folklore. He used the magic of words to take us into a wonderland. When I opened *Timeless Tales from Marwar*, I walked into his enchanted land all over again.

I came to the villages in Rajasthan in 1975 and was surrounded by storytellers. I was delighted. Their stories are in the 'oral tradition', not written down but narrated. Every retelling adds textures, from one generation to the next for hundreds of years. I heard them with great interest but could not remember them all. There was no book I could refer to, till I came across *Batan ri Phulwari*.

Bijji almost stepped out of his stories. He wore a dhoti and a *bagtari* (a cross buttoned kurta), a pair of beautiful elegant *joothis* that adorned his feet, had two pens in his breast pocket, one green and one red. He was one of the wittiest and fun people I have ever met. He made me laugh and learn together.

His retelling of folk stories is simple but layered. They talk of different castes, the poor, of people who live in havelis, *bastis, jhopris*, across different time periods. He speaks through the sun, the stars, the clouds, the peacock and the raindrops during monsoon. The superiority of the tiger is cleverly undermined by the jackal, and the arrogance of the bad man is turned on its head by the poor man's intelligence. We hear birds speak, while people have conversations with ghosts. Big ideas like poverty, untouchability and greed for wealth become simple. His style is witty. He uses satire, laughter and humour. Bijji makes the tale come alive—an attribute of a great writer. Although the stories are of days gone by, the messages are important for us even today. They are universal and for all time.

Bijji's stories are part of my mind. They pop up when I have to illustrate a point, or whenever there is a human condition that echoes his marvellous tales. The stories do not tell you what to think nor do, they just nudge you to think clearly, with compassion and wisdom. We all owe Bijji a great debt for keeping our cultural narrative alive with wisdom and humour. *Batan ri Phulwari* with the

Arabian Nights, and the myths we all know and love, will live forever. In translating it from the Rajasthani, Vishes Kothari continues 'the Bijji tradition' of retelling the stories, taking it beyond Rajasthan, into the timeless zone across nations.

I invite you to open *Timeless Tales from Marwar* and dip into any story.

My favourite? Every one of them is special. I leave you to discover yours.

December 2019
Mazdoor Kisan Shakti
Sangathan, Rajasthan

Aruna Roy
(with anecdotes from
Shankar Singh)

The Tale of Tell and Don't-Tell

'But there are other forms of this story that are popular. These are related to the sequence of telling stories. The children of Borunda told us that when they sat down to hear stories from their mothers, grandmothers or other elderly women at night, then it would be the story of Tell and Don't-Tell with which the telling would start.'

—Komal Kothari, ethnomusicologist

A king had two queens. He had died, but his queens lived. One queen was named Tell, and the other Don't-Tell.

Now, when Tell would tell the clouds to pour, they would rumble with thunder, flash with lightning and pour forth the nectar of their hearts. And when Don't-Tell would tell the clouds not to, the clouds would stay quiet and a drought would befall.

When Tell would tell the spring to spring, greenery would burst forth and colourful flowers would bloom. And when Don't-Tell would tell the spring not to, then it would become icy-cold and all the trees would wither.

On Tell's telling, the sun would glow and shine, the moon would gleam, the stars would sparkle, the rivers would flow and the waterfalls would gush. And on Don't-Tell's telling, the sun would eclipse the moon and the moon would eclipse the sun, dark nights would come to pass, the stars would break apart and the waterfalls would dry out.

From the mouth of Tell would pour flowers and pearls. From the mouth of Don't-Tell would shed embers and stones.

'So children, tell me, do you like Tell or Don't-Tell?'

'We like Tell! We like Tell!'

The Winds of Time

'. . . But has any Russian author become known for his writing in French? One gets known for one's work in one's mother tongue. Like the pens of Gogol, of Leo Tolstoy, of Dostoevsky, of Maxim Gorky . . . In my heart too, there rose a desire to write in my mother tongue, Rajasthani; a desire so strong that I would not feel like writing even a letter in any other language . . . And by 1958–59, I had sworn that if I was to write, it must be in my mother tongue, Rajasthani.'

—Vijaydan Detha, fondly known as Bijji

No god like time.
No brother like time.
No journey like time.
No shadow like time.

No doer like time.
No undoer like time.
The drums of time.
The *leela*[1] of time.
Tales of time. Change with time.

Once, in the lap of a certain time, there was a happy and content village. And though they all had their homes, they would all gather at the same spot to chit-chat each day. As soon as the elders and the men would finish their meals, they would come and sit around together and talk about their family lives. Ancient stories would fly around. When they heard something to laugh at, they laughed. When they heard something to be pained at, they sighed. No one had even learnt the words of untruth and trickery! They said the truth and heard the truth.

Mellow hearths simmered in every home, but there were no fires in any corner! Simple dreams and simple *kaam*.[2] The earth below, and above, Ram! Their needs, only as much as can fit into the palm of the hand! Bread for the stomach. Water to drink. Clothes to wear. A home to live in. Every home was lit up even before the sun rose in the sky!

---

[1] Sorcery or magic; play
[2] Work

In this village, there was a farmer who tilled the lands of a landlord. The farmer tried hard to get the landlord to take a share of the produce as rent, but the landlord would just not agree. When the farmer insisted and insisted, the landlord said that he had a lot of land already. He wouldn't carry the land on his head with him after his death! Plough, sow, earn and eat! The farmer took this dispute to the Panchayat. However, all the people in the village sided with the landlord.

One day, the farmer started digging a spot in the field, and one by one, he discovered seven pots full of gold mohurs! Without any delay, he harnessed his cart, loaded it with this treasure and headed straight towards the landlord's home.

When the landlord saw the cart approaching from a distance, he got annoyed at the farmer. After he'd said a clear 'no' to taking rent, how dare the farmer bring a cart full of produce? He would teach the farmer a nice lesson! How could he even think of going against the village's decision? But when the landlord saw the pots in the cart, his anger cooled down. Smiling, he said, 'What is this new headache you have brought along?'

Also smiling, the farmer said, 'You insisted on not taking a share of the produce and got by, but this headache you will have to accept!'

When the lids of the pots were removed and he saw the glittering gold mohurs, the landlord asked in surprise, 'Did these mohurs grow in the fields instead of bajri?'[1]

---

[1] Bajra, a type of millet

The farmer knew that if they spoke of things growing in the fields, the landlord would again refuse to take rent. So he promptly corrected the landlord, 'Has there ever been a field where mohurs grow, pray tell me? I found these seven pots while digging, so please accept them!'

The landlord felt a spasm of anger. He said, '*You* found them, so *you* keep them! Why did you bring them here?'

The farmer replied sternly, 'The land is *yours*! That is why I brought them. Don't you glare at me! Don't waste my time, I have lots of work! Quietly accept these pots so I can get rid of them. You had it your way on the rent. Isn't that enough?'

The landlord put on a pretence of affection and said, 'Look, you are again being unjust! You found the pots while labouring in the fields, so how can I accept them? My brain is still in its place!'

'If your brain was in its place, you wouldn't have said a flat "no" like this! Such a silly thing, even a child wouldn't say! When the field is yours, then the pots must be yours too! What's there to argue so much about?'

The landlord said agitatedly, 'It seems you alone have become the judge of everyone's brains in this entire village! Hearing such ridiculousness, the people of the village will laugh at you, make fun of you! Anyway, I won't say no to setting up a Panchayat to resolve this matter once and for all.'

The farmer stomped and replied loudly, 'Why would *you* say no? It is *I* who says no! No one does justice to a poor person! There should at least be a matter to call a Panchayat!'

The landlord snapped, 'What do you mean? How is this not a matter for a Panchayat? That day in the fields, when you got a cut on your legs, did anything happen to my legs? Tell me, when you work in my fields in the monsoons, if lightning strikes you, will you die or will I die?'

'If lightning strikes me, then only I will die.'

'But since the land is mine, I should die! Now tell me, if while working in the fields, you get bitten by a snake, will the poison kill you or me? Tell me! Tell me!'

'Now you stop these topsy-turvy riddles! I trusted you and came here straightaway. I know I will not get justice from the Panchayat.'

'Then why call for a Panchayat? Quietly take these pots to your home! I won't say a word to anyone, anywhere!'

'You can say lots of words,' the farmer shot back. 'I am not scared of anyone! Even with a borrowed face, I would still feel a tinge of shame in saying such silly things as you are uttering right now! How can I take *your* wealth to *my* home? You and your pots should sort it out! I am leaving this cart here and going back to the fields. In all this time spent here, I could have finished half the digging. I have no time for pointless arguments!' The farmer turned around and hurried away.

The landlord called after him, 'Look, don't just leave this argument unfinished and go. You will repent it!'

'So be it!' came the reply.

The landlord was beside himself with rage. But if the farmer would just not listen, what could he have done?

An hour, hour and a half or so after nightfall, the Panchayat was called. When the cause of the dispute was heard, the panch asked the farmer a question. 'Did these pots come out of the fields on their own, or did you dig them out?'

'Of course I dug them out! When have pots jumped out of a field on their own?'

The panch smiled and said, 'Then you have solved the problem with your own words—the fruits of your toil must accrue to you!'

But that obstinate farmer still did not agree. He started the same arguments in the Panchayat. 'But the land is not mine! My heart just cannot accept the idea of pocketing the wealth dug up in the land of another!'

The panch said, 'It is not up to us to make your heart agree. What is up to us is to do justice, which we have done. No one owns the earth, the water or the wind. If you are so honest, then you should never breathe the air that blows over the land of another.'

'If you so suggest, then I won't.'

'But why would we suggest something so silly! Listen to us—till we find out who buried the mohurs there, you watch over them.'

'And what will this watching over cost me? It would be like selling my sleep and buying worry! Ram knows who buried these mohurs and with what hope! Either you come up with a just decision or else I will go and deposit this in the treasury of the raj.'

'We have given a decision as per our understanding,' said the panch. 'If you don't agree, it's your wish!'

The farmer shot back, 'When you know nothing about justice, why even wash your face and land up here to pretend to dispense it?' Saying this, that stubborn farmer harnessed his cart and went straight to the Raj Durbar.

The raja carefully heard everything and said, 'I became the king to protect people's lives and wealth. So what right do I have to snatch your wealth away? You've gone through all this trouble in vain. The panches of your village have not done you any injustice. You take these pots and happily go home. Your toil, your fruit!'

Hearing the raja say this, the farmer's face fell. He had gone there with some other hope. Utterly disappointed, he said, 'I won't agree to your decision even in death. And what would I even do with these mohurs? They'll just take up space! If it doesn't upset you, then I will take the panches to the farm and have these pots buried exactly where I found them.'

In the cusp of that age of goodness, the king was just like his people. A smile appeared on his lips. 'Your wish!'

Finally, things happened exactly as per the farmer's wishes. At sunrise on the third day, the people of this village stood around and watched as the farmer buried those seven pots in the same spot in the fields with his own hands!

And the winds of change blew without pause on the slopes of time.

And they kept blowing! Caught up in the gusts of those winds, neither did the farmer endure, nor those villagers, nor that raja! A new generation appeared in the lap of time. A new generation with new blood.

In those new winds, the memories of the days of yore still lingered on. One day, the landlord's grown-up son went the farmer's son and said, 'My forefathers were silly, but I am not at all silly!'

Before he could say anything further, the farmer's son's reply stopped him in his tracks. 'You are not at all silly! But I am just as silly as my forefathers!' the farmer's son said with a smile.

'Yes, that you are silly, I know! Isn't that why in the dead of night you dug out those pots that were buried in the fields and then sneaked them back to your home?'

The farmer's son thought to himself that the landlord's son had surely surveyed the fields already. But the landlord's son would have found those pots only if they were there! He had had the good sense to take all the pots home just a week ago. Else, today, he would not have been able to lay his hands on a single mohur! If he cowed down now, the matter might get out of hand. So, without hesitation, he replied, 'Why, what is there to ask? I don't till this land for free, do I? I pay a third of the harvest as rent. If while digging the fields, a snake bites me, then hardship will befall *my* kids. No harm will come to you. I took home the wealth I dug up with my toil. What is there to hide in this?'

The two argued a lot, but the landlord's son was not able to achieve much. Finally, he left with a threat: 'Let's see how you are able to digest the wealth that was buried in *my* fields!'

'What is left to digest? It has already been digested! Sir, one cannot go far on wealth snatched from others. One can get by only on the fruit of one's own toil!'

Eyes red with rage, the landlord's son went and screamed in front of the villagers. Such a juicy panchayati[1] rarely comes by! The tummy and the palm would be greased for many a day! The landlord's son called the panches to his home and how he pampered them! When the farmer's son found out, he too called them home and warmed their hands. And so, the view of the panches changed!

The Panchayat would be called every night. A lot of screaming and shouting would go on till midnight. Soon, the entire village became divided into two camps, with half the panches on the side of the landlord's son and the other

[1] A panchayati refers to a case or a matter that a panchayat deliberates on.

half on the side of the farmer's son. How badly that string got entangled! But there was no shortcoming in the greed of the panches.

After many days of wracking their brains, the panches decided to split the mohurs in the way the harvest was split between the men, but the farmer's son would not agree. He had the power of those golden pieces of sun! And so, again, he called the panches to his home and pampered them. And how! Suddenly, the side of the landlord's son lost. The spineless tongues bent the other way! The poor landlord's son had spent money and lost despite it!

And again, the winds of change blew without pause. Countless leaves withered and countless new buds sprouted forth. The water of countless rivers joined the seas. Many a sun rose up in the sky and set on the horizon. Another generation went its way. And the new blood pulsing in the veins of a new generation rose into its heart. In those new winds, memories of old days lingered.

The landlord's grown-up grandson arrived at the farmer's grandson's house with his sword unsheathed. The farmer's grandson heard his shouts and came out with his own weapon. When screaming and arguing didn't resolve things, the landlord's grandson felt a fire rage from his head to his heel. Filled with fury, he brought his sword down on the neck of the farmer's grandson with force. Like chopping off the top of a carrot or a radish, the sword cleaved straight through the neck! The head rolled and fell at his feet!

Hearing the screams of their brother's wife, the two younger brothers of the farmer's grandson came out running—each holding a long sword. The middle brother brought his sword down on the landlord's grandson's neck and hacked half of it off his body. Fountains of blood soaked the earth. For the first time ever, the land of the village had a *mandana*[1] painted in blood instead of sweat!

The Panchayat congregated and went to the raja. As soon as the King heard of the buried wealth, his face turned purple with rage. All buried treasure belonged to the raj! On the command of the king, each of the Panchayat members was sentenced to twenty-one beatings of a shoe. Then the riders of the raj set out to the farmer's house, seized all seven pots and brought them back to the treasury!

Such were the winds of change. The peace of that happy and content village was destroyed. And the village was engulfed by the flames of change! Ram knows if those flames will die out or if they will not die out.

Tales of time. Change with time.

---

[1] A type of rangoli or mural art made on floors or courtyards in Rajasthan

Jheentiya

'But [once I had decided to write in Rajasthani] how was I to acquire the skill of writing in it? . . . Tired, I confided in Babasa [Goverdhanlalji Kabra]. At first, he said, "What silliness is this? You were writing well in Hindi. Readers were reading your work and praising you. Where will you find readers for Rajasthani? . . . But [if you have decided] then you must leave Jodhpur. Go back to your village Borunda. The stories that, on their strength alone, have survived in the memories of people—nurture them with your craft. If you respect them, then they will ensure you are respected. Make the illiterate folk of the village your gurus . . . The voices of women are richer than those of men. In their voices dwell countless sayings, songs and stories, like diamonds and pearls. You will never reach the bottom of this treasure."'

—Bijji

In a village lived a widowed mother Who had one child who was named Jheentiya. Jheentiya was young in years, but his brain whirred like the wheel of a well. One day, he said to his mother, 'Ma, ma, I'm going to my *nanire*.'[1]

Ma said, 'Beta, you're still young. The way to your nanire is overrun with animals that will eat you up. Once you grow up, go then.'

Jheentiya requested his mother a lot, but she just wouldn't listen.

Then one day, Jheentiya came up with a clever scheme. To tease his mother, he said, 'Ae, ma, my father has been dead for twelve years now . . . For whom do you put this kajal in your eyes?' The mother ran to smack him. Jheentiya escaped and began sprinting to his nanire.

On the way, he ran into a crow. He saw Jheentiya and cawed, 'Jheentiya, Jheentiya! I will eat you!' But fear wasn't something that could even wander near Jheentiya.

'Kagla[2] bhai, Kagla bhai, why eat me like this!' said Jheentiya. 'Let me go to my nanire. Let me drink doodh malai.[3] Let me eat dahi rotiyo.[4] Let me become *moto-tajo*.[5] Then eat me!'

---

[1] Mother's natal home
[2] Crow
[3] Milk and cream
[4] Dahi and rotis
[5] *mota-tazaa* in Hindi, meaning 'fat' or 'plump'

The crow replied, 'Who knows! You may come or you may not come!'

Jheentiya answered, 'Can this even be? I give you my word!' Saying so, he ran farther along the way to his nanire.

Soon, he ran into a jackal. 'Jheentiya, Jheentiya! I will eat you!' But fear wasn't something Jheentiya knew.

'Lunki[1] bai,[2] Lunki bai, why eat me like this!' he said. 'Let me go to my nanire. Let me drink doodh malai. Let me eat dahi rotiyo. Let me become moto-tajo. Then eat me!'

The jackal said, 'Who knows! You may come or you may not come!'

Jheentiya answered, 'Can this even be? I give you my word.' And so, he ran farther along the way.

Soon, he ran into a fox. 'Jheentiya, Jheentiya! I will eat you!' barked the fox.

'Siyal[3] mama,[4] Siyal mama, why eat me like this!'

'Then how?' asked the flummoxed fox.

'Let me go to my nanire. Let me drink doodh malai. Let me eat dahi rotiyo. Let me become moto-tajo. Then eat me!'

The fox said, 'Who knows! You may come or you may not come!'

---

[1] Jackal
[2] Sister
[3] Fox
[4] Uncle; mother's brother; also called Mamoji

'Can this even be? I give you my word,' said Jheentiya. And so, he ran farther along the way to his nanire.

Soon, he ran into a cheetah. 'Jheentiya, Jheentiya! I will eat you!'

'Cheetah mama, cheetah mama,' began Jheentiya, 'why eat me like this! Let me go to my nanire. Let me drink doodh malai. Let me eat dahi rotiyo. Let me become moto-tajo. Then eat me!'

'Who knows! You may come or you may not come!'

Jheentiya was ready with an answer. 'Can this even be? I give you my word.' And so, he scurried farther along the way.

In this way, Jheentiya gave all four animals the slip and managed to reach his nanire safe and sound. Everyone there showered him with affection. He had four mamis[1] who lived there. One of them said, 'My dear bhanecha,[2] stay with me.' The other said, 'My loving nephew, come stay with me.'

'Don't fight, all of you,' replied Jheentiya. 'I'll stay with the mami who has lots of cows that give lots of milk.' Now, only the youngest mami had milk-giving cows, so Jheentiya went to stay with her. And oh! How the youngest aunt pampered Jheentiya! Fresh, rich, creamy and frothy milk

---

[1] Mama's wife
[2] Nephew

with honey. Choorma[1] mushy with cow's ghee! And even as one watched, Jheentiya grew tall and strong. He began to glow from head to toe!

One day, Jheentiya asked his youngest mami, 'Mami, what is the deal with you, Ae? You go to sleep in the stores but are found in the kitchen; you go to sleep in the kitchen but are found in the aangan.[2] When you sleep in the aangan, you are found at the doorway; when you sleep in the doorway, you are found in the gardens; when you sleep in the gardens, you are found by the bank of the pond. Can't make head or tail of this strangeness . . . Tell me the truth.'

'My dear nephew, my head is squirming with lice,' she replied. 'They drag me around! When I sleep in the stores, they drag me to the kitchen; when I sleep in the kitchen, they drag me into the aangan. I'm quite sick of these lice! What to do?'

Jheentiya went running to a carpenter. He had a fine-toothed comb readied and combed his mami's hair with it. Mounds of squirming lice fell out! Jheentiya kept on combing her hair. And heaps and heaps of lice kept falling

---

[1] A traditional Rajasthani dish made of crushed wheat flour dumplings with ghee.

[2] Inner courtyard

out. He pulled out every last lice. Soon mami's head began to feel as light as air. She blessed Jheentiya many times. After the lice were removed, his mami was always found where she went to sleep!

Jheentiya filled these lice into a pouch and went to the edge of the village. Here, under a large khejdi[1] tree were resting some buffaloes. Jheentiya emptied the pouch on the buffaloes. As soon as the lice began biting the buffaloes, they began to flee from there!

A lion was lying in wait to hunt those buffaloes. When the lion saw the buffaloes fleeing, he began chasing after them. As he was running, a sharp thorn pricked his foot. The buffaloes escaped, leaving the lion far behind.

Fear could not wander even close to Jheentiya. His brain began whirring like the wheel of a well. He went near the lion and said, 'Mamoji, greetings. How come you stopped in the midst of the chase?'

'A sharp thorn has pierced my feet,' the lion grumbled. 'I can't even move an inch. These legs have made my body limp. Now, Jheentiya, if you pluck out this thorn, I'll breathe a sigh of relief.'

'I can surely pluck out the thorn, but what if you eat me up afterwards?'

The lion quickly replied, 'No, ae, no! You will do me a good turn and I will eat you up? The race of lions isn't that lowly!'

---

[1] The state tree of Rajasthan

Jheentiya answered, 'Low or high, once the body becomes fit and fine, one gets blinded by the pangs of hunger. I'm not going to poke my head into the den of death.'

When the lion pleaded with Jheentiya and tears welled up in his eyes, Jheentiya took pity on him. *We'll think of a solution when the problem arises*, he thought to himself. And so, he went to the blacksmith and bought a pair of tweezers. He placed the lion's paw on his knee and plucked out the thorn. Some blood started to ooze out. Jheentiya quickly sprinkled some fine sand on the wound.

As soon as the thorn was extracted, the lion felt at ease. He patted Jheentiya's back with his paw and praised him. 'Jheentiya, I'm dying of hunger. Do me one more favour. Get me some prey here. The very light in my eyes dims from the hunger in my tummy. If you help me, I will tell you of a buried treasure . . . ' Uttering these words, the lion plonked himself down.

Jheentiya again felt some pity. 'Mamoji, you sit in the shade of the khejdi. I will get some prey in no time at all.'

Jheentiya began wandering the jungle barefoot in search of prey. Soon he reached a pond. He spotted a donkey grazing along its bank. He went near the donkey and said, 'Mamoji, greetings.'

The donkey raised his head, gazed at Jheentiya and said, 'Bhaya,[1] since when are you my nephew?'

---

[1] Brother; popularly used to address a young man

Jheentiya answered, 'You have a fair sister; I'm her little son.'

The donkey nodded. 'Now I recognize you! You are well, no?'

'All the better after seeing you,' said Jheentiya with a smile. But, mamoji, how come you graze alone? Are you still unmarried?'

The donkey sighed deeply. 'Doesn't look like that's happening in this birth!'

'Why do you worry even as I live? I have set out to search for a match—for a maiden. A young beauty. Sharp-nosed, doe-eyed, saffron-hued, the home abounds with brothers and sisters. Both parents still living. They will give lots of nice gifts and a better dowry. Now, why would I look for another groom while my mamoji lives? Come, I'll get you to take the *feras*[1] straightaway.'

The prospect of getting married made the donkey's eyes red with delight. Happiness made his eyes turn scarlet. 'Mamoji, your eyes have turned blood-red,' said Jheentiya. 'They glow like embers! The maiden's sisters will flee in fright as soon as they spot you. We don't want to miss this chance. Tie a band around your eyes and come with me; we'll get you married right away.'

That donkey, eager to get married, did exactly as Jheentiya asked. He tied a band over his eyes and began following the boy.

---

1 Also known as pheras, meaning 'the ambulations taken around the holy fire in a Hindu wedding ceremony'

As soon as Jheentiya came near the lion, he told the donkey, 'Your mother-in-law will welcome you and pull your nose,[1] so don't you be scared.' He then caught the donkey by the ear and nudged him nearer to the lion. The lion grabbed the other ear with his paws. As a spasm of pain ran down the donkey's body, he jerked free from their hold and fled from there as fast as he could. He breathed only once he'd reached the bank of the pond again.

Dejected, the lion remained standing there. He could not even chase a donkey. Berating the lion, Jheentiya said, 'Shame on you! Can't even hunt a donkey!'

'Now, you can jeer at me all you like, but I'm dying of hunger. Get him back once more, and this time I'll rather die than let him go.'

And so, Jheentiya returned to the bank of that very pond. He found the donkey at the same spot. 'What, Mamoji, such a loss of face for me in front of so many people! You fled from there! You could have checked with me once at least.'

The donkey said, 'Bhaya, you had my ear ripped apart! It's still bleeding. Is that a sasu[2] or a demoness? I don't want to marry the daughter of such a woman! How will I live with her? I don't want your big dowry.'

Laughing, Jheentiya said, 'Mamoji, that was your sisters-in-law piercing your ears! They're gifting you a

---

[1] A wedding ritual where the bride's mother welcomes the groom by pulling his nose
[2] Mother-in-law

22

chain of a hundred tolas[1] of gold and earrings worth twenty tolas! Now, there will surely be some pain while getting ears pierced, right? But you ran away. That's why your ear got cut. Come quickly now! The auspicious hour is passing!'

And so, the donkey again followed Jheentiya with a band around his eyes.

This time the lion was alert. As soon as the donkey came near, the lion brought down his paw with full force on the donkey's head. The donkey collapsed there and then. As he lay taking his last breath, he could only utter, 'Bhanecha, marriage . . . !'

'One wedding is done, another awaits,' chuckled Jheentiya. The lion struck again with his paw and the donkey finished his vows there itself.

Seeing the donkey dead, vultures began circling above. Those hungry vultures tried a lot, but the lion was guarding his prize. They didn't dare alight on the ground. Jheentiya saw the hungry vultures circling and felt pity for them. His brain began whirring like the wheel of a well. He quickly thought up a plan. When the hungry lion started to eat the carcass, Jheentiya said, 'Mamoji, why eat like this?'

The lion asked, 'Then how must I eat?'

'You are the king of the forest. You must eat as a king does! Rinse your mouth, say your prayers, bathe yourself and then eat as befits a king.'

---

[1] A unit of weight in India that is used to measure gold; 1 tola equals 11.6 grams

The lion agreed with Jheentiya. 'I'll say my prayers and return; you keep watch for me.'

'Come back soon,' said Jheentiya. As soon as the lion left, Jheentiya plucked out the donkey's eyes, ears, heart and brain and threw it to the hungry vultures.

When the lion returned after saying his prayers, Jheentiya was sitting quietly under the khejdi tree. The lion bent to bite into the donkey's flesh, when he noticed that its eyes were missing. The lion turned and said, 'Jheentiya, where are this donkey's eyes?'

Jheentiya replied, 'Mamoji, if he had eyes, would he have returned to you a second time?'

The lion said, 'Jheentiya, this donkey doesn't have ears only!'

'Mamoji, if he had ears, would he not have heard you roar? Why would he have returned a second time to die like this?'

Then the lion said, 'Jheentiya, this donkey doesn't have a brain only!'

Jheentiya again answered, 'Mamoji, he was brainless! Else why would he have returned to get married? If he had a brain, what would he come to you for?'

The lion said, 'Jheentiya, this donkey doesn't have a heart only!'

'Mamoji, if he had a heart, would he not have faced up to you? Only lions have hearts, and that's why they can hunt! If other animals had hearts, wouldn't lions die of hunger?'

The lion was convinced. He ate to his heart's fill. Once full, he said, 'Let's go, Jheentiya. Let me now tell you about the buried treasure and keep my word.'

The lion began digging with his paws near a bush. And soon handed Jheentiya an urn full of diamonds and pearls. 'Don't forget to invite me to your wedding,' said the lion. 'I'll come with the maayra.'[1]

Jheentiya guffawed. 'After this donkey's wedding today, the next wedding will be mine!'

The lion also laughed *dag-dag* at Jheentiya's joke. Patting his back, he said, 'Jheentiya, your brain moves so fast, re.'

And so, Jheentiya returned to his mami's house with the urn full of diamonds and pearls.

He divided half the treasure between his four mamis and kept the other half for his Ma. He chuckled to his youngest mami, 'I sold your lice and bought these diamonds and pearls. Very costly! Costlier than your lice!'

One day, Jheentiya said to his aunt, 'Mami, now I should be heading back to Ma.'

'Why the haste? Stay some more days. You've come to your nanire! Return home a little later.'

---

[1] A wedding ritual where the mother of the bride or groom receives gifts of clothes and jewels from her brothers and their families

But once he'd decided, who could change Jheentiya's mind? 'Many friends wait for me on the way back home. I will have to go,' he said, continuing, 'Mami, have a *dhamki*[1] made for me. I'll sit in it and go home.'

And so, his aunt got a dhamki made for him. Then made Jheentiya sit inside it. Placed a flask of water inside. And a *katordaan*[2] of choorma.

Once he was inside, he said, 'Now, all you four aunts must blow air at the dhamki— all together.' And so, all the mamis blew at the same time. The barrel began to roll away. *Gud gud gud gud!* When he was hungry, Jheentiya had the choorma mushy with ghee. When he was thirsty, he had cool water from the flask.

Soon he encountered the same cheetah he had met before. The cheetah called out, 'Dhamki, dhamki. Have you seen Jheentiya, ae?'

Sitting inside, Jheentiya munched on the choorma mushy with ghee. Had a sip of cool water. Then, so that the cheetah would not recognize him, he said in Hindi:

'Kiska Jheentiya, kiska tam?
Chal meri dhamki, dhamaak-a-dham!
'Who is Jheentiya, who are you?
Come on my dhamki, go dhamaak-a-dham!'

---

[1] Barrel
[2] A round box, which is usually used as a food container

And it rolled. And the dhamki didn't stop while going uphill nor downhill. It thought nothing of boulders or of ditches. It went on rolling and rolling. *Gud gud gud gud!*

Soon, he encountered the same fox again. The fox barked, 'Dhamki, dhamki. Have you seen Jheentiya, ae?'

Sitting inside, Jheentiya ate some choorma soaked with ghee. Took a sip of cool water. Then, so that the fox would not recognize him, he said in Hindi:

'Kiska Jheentiya, kiska tam?

Chal meri dhamki, dhamaak-a-dham!'

And so the dhamki rolled on. It didn't stop while going uphill nor downhill. It thought nothing of boulders or of ditches. It went on rolling and rolling. *Gud gud gud gud!*

Very soon, he encountered the same jackal again. The jackal said, 'Dhamki, dhamki. Have you seen Jheentiya, ae?'

Sitting inside, Jheentiya munched on some choorma soaked in ghee. Drank some cool water from the flask. Then, so that the jackal would not recognize him, he said in Hindi:

'Kiska Jheentiya, kiska tam?

Chal meri dhamki, dhamaak-a-dham!'

And so the dhamki rolled on. It didn't stop while going uphill nor downhill. It thought nothing of boulders or of ditches. It went on rolling and rolling. *Gud gud gud gud!*

Next, he encountered the same crow again. The crow cawed, 'Dhamki, dhamki. Have you seen Jheentiya, ae?'

Sitting inside, he munched on some choorma soaked in ghee. Then gulped some cool water from the flask. Then, so that the crow would not recognize him, he spoke in Hindi again:

'Kiska Jheentiya, kiska tam?

Chal meri dhamki, dhamaak-a-dham!'

But the crow got suspicious. Somehow, he was sure that it was Jheentiya inside. He pecked so hard at the dhamki that it broke. Jheentiya emerged smiling, for fear wasn't something he knew.

The crow flew high up and began cawing loudly. 'Found Jheentiya! Found Jheentiya!' The cheetah, the fox and the jackal came running and surrounded Jheentiya. But Jheentiya stood there fearlessly. As the wheel of a well whirs, so did his brain. Quickly, he came up with a clever plan.

The four animals said at the same time, 'Jheentiya, today we will not leave you. We will eat you. You have come back mighty moto-tajo from your nanire.'

'Eat me by all means,' Jheentiya began. 'But not like this!'

'Then how?' they asked.

Jheentiya had an answer ready, of course. 'Get chillies. Get salt. Get lots of acid. Fry the spices in the acid and then fry me. Then eat me! What taste! If you eat me as humans eat, I will have a good afterlife.'

The animals then left, leaving the crow to keep watch. The cheetah, the fox and the jackal went separate ways and soon returned with powdered chillies, ground salt and a pot of acid. 'Jheentiya, we don't know how to ready the spices. You do it.'

This was exactly what Jheentiya wanted. Promptly, he took the pot in his hand and said, 'What's there to think about in this? I'll make it right now.'

Jheentiya added the salt and chillies to the pot of acid. He took a stick and mixed it all up. The four were sitting around and watching, when Jheentiya said, 'Put a little in your eyes and see. Tell me how it tastes. Tell me, it's not over-salted, no?'

One said, 'Put it in my eyes first!'

The other screamed, 'No, in my eyes first!'

Seeing them fight, Jheentiya calmly spoke, 'Be patient. Why such haste? When your turn comes, I'll serve each of you. You are all equal for me.' And so, the four sat down, eyes wide open. Quickly, Jheentiya threw the spice and acid mixture into their eyes. As soon as the mixture went into their eyes, their eyes burst! All four began screaming and crying at the top of their lungs. 'Our eyes! It's too spicy! Our eyes! What a horrid thing to happen!'

The crow tried to fly away from there, but Jheentiya caught him by the wings and pushed him into the acid mixture. The crow instantly melted. Jheentiya then poured the mix on the heads of the remaining three. The three screamed, 'Jheentiya! The spices are too strong, re!'

And all three animals fled! One said, 'I will flee first!'

The other screamed, 'I will flee first!'

Jheentiya laughed and sat in his dhamki again.

'Chal meri dhamki, dhamaak-a-dham!'

And so the dhamki rolled on. It didn't stop while going uphill nor downhill. It thought nothing of boulders or of ditches. It went on rolling and rolling. *Gud gud gud gud!*

Soon it stopped at the doorway to his home. Ma was eagerly waiting for Jheentiya, and as soon as she saw him, she gave him a tight hug. 'How fat you've returned from your nanire! Lest the evil eye fall on you, let me tie this black thread around you.' Saying this, she spat on him to ward off the evil eye.

Jheentiya sold the diamonds and pearls and built a palace that soared into the sky. Celebrated his wedding with great dhoom dhaam. Promptly sent the wedding invite to his lion mama. The mama gifted five similar urns of diamonds and pearls in the maayra. Everyone in the realm feasted on five delicacies. The lion mama's name became well known throughout the world. Jheentiya lived with his mother in peace and happiness for many years.

End of chit, end of chat,
The neighbour's got really fat.
The horses did a poo,
Which the potter took.
The potter made pots
And placed them by the river.
Coming-going, the cows broke them.
Why re, milkman, don't use your stick, why?
What to do, Ma doesn't give rotis, that's why.

Why ae, Ma, no rotis, why?
What to do, the bahus don't grind flour, that's why.
Why re, bahus don't grind flour, why?
What to do, the guests won't leave, that's why.
Why re, guests won't leave, why?
What to do, the rain pours, that's why.
Why re, rain, you pour, why?
What to do, the peacocks call, that's why.
Why re, peacocks, you call, why?
What to do, the clouds thunder, that's why.
Why re, clouds, you thunder, why?
What to do, the lightning flashes, that's why.
Why re, lightning, you flash, why?
What to do, the story sizzles, that's why!

The Learning of Toil

'In old handwritten manuscripts, there is a story of about a page and a half. Which I extended . . . added many a twist to the conversation between Raja Bhoj, the old woman and the Pandit . . . one of the foremost tales in the world. How else could I pay off the debts I owe to my gurus?'

—Bijji

It was the reign of Raja Bhoj in Ujjain Nagari. Widely loved, ocean of knowledge, fount of wisdom, patron of the arts. Merciful, righteous, protector of the realm! The people of the kingdom respected him like their father. Anyone could approach him without fear and talk to him; the raja would meet them as equals. He would roam the kingdom alone and find out about the people's pain, erase their suffering and fulfil their wishes. At his court, poets, intellectuals, singers and men of letters were greatly respected. The court of Raja Bhoj in Ujjain Nagari was the centre of an unparalleled gathering of intellectuals. Even the birds and animals were wise and learned. Every day, the durbar was held and there were debates and discussions. The glow of the raja's name spread to every home.

One day, the raja asked his pandits and intellectuals, 'Where can one find the Garden of Knowledge?'

All the poets and intellectuals who fed off the grains of the court, replied that of course it was none other than the court itself! The foremost place of knowledge was the Raj Durbar, followed by the fortresses and castles, and then the havelis and mansions. 'Where there is power and wealth, there follow knowledge and artistry. And without wisdom and learning, wealth and power cannot be amassed,' they replied. 'And so, the luckless poor lack wisdom and knowledge and hence lack wealth and power.' All the intellectuals said the same thing in different-different ways, giving different-different examples. Intellectuals of such stature were all saying it with so much conviction that Raja Bhoj had to believe them!

A gardener was listening to these discussions quietly. Finally, he said, 'Annadata[1] . . . !'

Raja Bhoj cut him off. 'Again the same thing! I have explained to you people a thousand times that I am not the Annadata, *you* are! I am just a shepherd.'

---

[1] Provider of grain

The gardener accepted his mistake and said that it would take time to change this habit of generations. Then he said, 'I have become tired merely listening to these discussions about this Garden of Knowledge. Neither have my ears heard of such a thing nor have my eyes seen it. So it is pointless to argue about it. If you want to see a garden of the miracles of nature, come with me to my garden. I came to the Durbar to invite you.'

Accompanied by the Magh Pandit from his court, Raja Bhoj left instantly. The garden was five miles out of the city. The three of them reached the garden at midday. So many colours! So many scents! In the lap of that green earth danced many vibrant flowers. To see nature in such bounteous bloom was to make the gift of light to one's eyes meaningful! The raja got lost as his sight danced among the flowers in that garden. The Pandit kept reminding the raja of the time, so they finally started to head back. The gardener offered to accompany them on the way back, lest they lose their way, but the raja wouldn't hear of it.

After about a mile and a half, the King and his priest lost their way. Surely they had not crossed these fields of wheat on their way to the garden earlier! Helpless, they looked around. At the edge of the field, they saw a *dokri*[1] standing. White hair. Completely bent. Trembling head. Guarding

---

[1] An old woman

her fields from birds. They went near her and folded their hands in greeting. 'Live long, sons,' she said.

The raja asked her, 'Ma, where does this road go?'

She smiled before she answered. Her toothless smile lit up her face like starlight. Then she raised her head to look at the raja and said, 'Beta, this road will stay where it is. But the travellers who walk on it come and go.'

Then she asked them, 'Beta, who are you?'

'We are travellers of the road.'

She said, 'Ni, beta. The travellers of the road are two others!'

This time, it was the Pandit who asked, 'And who are they?'

'One, the sun, and the other, the moon. They move across the sky, night and day. Don't stop for a second. They are the travellers. But tell me, who are you?'

They said, 'We are guests.'

She said, 'Ni, beta. The guests are two others. They are youth and wealth. They never stop for long. They are guests. But who are you?'

'We are *pardesis*.'[1]

'Ni, beta. The pardesis are two others. They are the wind and the *jeev*.[2] The jeev leaves and no one sees it go. And it is because of the wind that this body sustains. And

_____

[1] Foreigners
[2] Soul or being

35

no one can stop it from leaving. Both are invisible. No one sees them go, and once gone, they never return. They are called the pardesis. But beta, who are you?'

They said, 'We are poor men.'

'Ni, beta. The poor are two others. They are the calf of the cow and the unmarried daughter. The bull ploughs the soil of who it is sold to, and the daughter lives for who her parents marry her to. The poor are those who must live according to the whims of others. But beta, tell me, who are you?'

The raja was really enjoying listening to the dokri. Wanting to test her wisdom, he said, 'Ma, we are thugs.'

She shook her head. 'Ni, beta. The thugs are two others. They are the king and the moneylender. The farmer toils and labours, while the king measures and gobbles. The moneylender fudges his accounts and charges twenty-one instead of one. Who in this world can be a bigger thug than these two? They thug everyone and yet pass off as great men. But tell me the truth, who are you?'

'We are the inebriated.'

'Ni, beta. The inebriated are two others. One is the devotee and the other, the scholar. The intoxication of drink wears off with time. That is no true intoxication. The devotee is intoxicated by his faith, the scholar with knowledge. What sort of rubbish drunks are you!'

They said, 'We are liars!'

She said, 'Ni, beta. The liars are two others . . . They are the sadhu and the atheist. The sadhu says he knows God, and the atheist says there is no God. I think there are no bigger liars than these two. But you know neither truth nor falsehood. All you know is to play games with me, which you are still going on with. Ram-damned, at least now tell me, who are you?'

'We are tricksters.'

'Ni, beta. The tricksters are two others . . . They are beauty and the ego. However proud of them you might be, they trick you and leave you in old age. Toothless mouth, white hair, bent back, sagging breasts—is this any small trickery? In one's youth, one thinks one can pierce the skies, but in old age, one cannot even shoo away the flies on one's face. Seeing me, don't you see what these two tricksters have done to me? But tell me, who are you? It's almost evening and you still can't answer a simple question. *Who* are you?'

This dokri was challenging everything they said! Today, both the men had forgotten the way back home, but they had also forgotten the path of learning and wisdom. The woman had entangled them in such a web that they could see no way out. Their pride and arrogance of years were shattered in seconds! Where the intellectuals of the Court were saying the Garden of Knowledge was, and where it had turned out to be!

Raja Bhoj finally said, 'We are losers.'

The dokri still would not give up. With that same smugness, she said, 'Na, the losers are two others. One is the indebted, and the other is the tiller of the land. A man can bear the weight of a mountain on his head, but he collapses under the weight of debt. And the tiller moves his hands and legs as per the wishes of others for the sake of his stomach—who can be a bigger loser than him! Beta, in this world, these are the two losers. But who are you, tell me? I'm losing my patience now, but you're still not telling me the truth.'

After listening to the dokri's words, the raja felt no anger. Nor was the Pandit willing to give up. Who could be more tolerant than these two! Raja Bhoj said, 'We are the tolerant.'

The dokri had not been born on such a night as to let this pass without challenge. She said, 'Na, who would call you tolerant! The tolerant are two others. They are the earth and the tree. The earth bears the weight of sinners and those without karma. We tear her chest apart and sow our seeds, but she still won't destroy the seeds. We plough her chest, but she still fills our stores with grain. We dig deep pits into her heart, yet she gives us sweet water and hands us priceless wealth, such as diamonds, pearls and gold. We cast stones at a fruiting tree, but it still gives us sweet fruit. When cut, the trees give us light and cook our meals. Even when burnt, they provide. They are named tolerant. In the middle of all this talk with you, I forgot to guard my fields. The naughty birds are having a great time!' she said, as she let off a shot from her sling and came and stood by them again.

The raja still felt no anger at the dokri. Who else but a saint could bear so much! Thinking this, the raja said, 'Ma, we are sanyasis—the renouncers.'

'Na, the renouncers are two others. One is he who is satisfied, and the other, who does not know. The man who has no greed at all in this world—not of wealth, nor fame, nor God nor knowledge—it is he who is a renouncer. Either he who knows everything can be so satisfied, or he who knows nothing! These are the only two people in this world who can be called renouncers. Now, it is about to be evening and you are unable to answer such a small question. What fools are you?'

Now it seemed best to admit defeat to the dokri. Thinking this, the Pandit finally gave up and said, 'We are fools of the highest order.'

'After eating my head for so long, finally you tell me the truth! Indeed, in this world there are only two fools—the raja and the Magh Pandit. The most ordinary raja begins to think himself equal to God! And surrounds himself with sycophants, who use their empty gyan to feed this lie.'

She then turned to look at the raja and said, 'You are Raja Bhoj and this is the Magh Pandit. Beta, why did you feed me all this nonsense? Have I lived off the crumbs of the Raj Durbar and wasted all these years? I see with my eyes, hear with my ears and think for myself. Those who live off the crumbs of the Court do not think, hear or see for themselves. But beta, those who live off their own toil cannot afford to do so. Only those who eat for free can afford such folly.'

By now, the Pandit was annoyed with the old woman. He said, 'This is all just clever wordplay. I will ask her a question, and we will get to know her wisdom only if she can answer.'

The old woman started laughing and said, 'Whatever for? Whom must I prove my wisdom to? Those who must prove their learning to others have some selfish need to do so. I am content as I am. Even then, ask if you must. If I know, I will tell you. If I don't, I won't hesitate to say I don't know. This poor human being—how much can one know of this endless universe? Only the illusion of knowing . . .'

Sonal Bai

'When collecting folk tales, one question that confronts
us is what are the occasions when these stories are
told? . . . Two-three occasions are clear. If these are
the *vrat kathas*[1] of women, then they are told on the
designated day of the vrat itself . . . In the same way,
when a grandmother or ma tells bedtime stories [to
children] on pleasant nights while going to sleep.
Other than these two occasions, when are folk stories
told? . . . One form which appears is its exemplary
use. Which is during conversation, one uses a story to
prove one's point . . . These stories have the form of a
kahaavat.[2] Then there are stories for which gatherings
are held. We found two forms of this type in the village.

---

[1] Vrat means 'fast'. Vrat kathas are stories narrated on the day of the fast.
[2] A meaningful saying or proverb

First, we found castes of ravs and bhats,[1] who along with maintaining genealogies also tell stories. They use . . . artful style, colourful language, tonal variations and emotionally charged ways of storytelling . . . In the same way, there are also other specialists among the people who will tell stories . . . In the winter, people will gather around a fire and stories will be told . . . Also when people water their fields at night . . . '

—Komal Kothari

In a village, there lived a farmer who had a very beautiful daughter. Who was named Sonal Bai, for the hair on her head was of pure gold. Sonal's mother took full-full care of her daughter's priceless hair and would go to great lengths to keep it safe. Before Sonal would go swimming in the lake with her friends, Ma would count her hair. When Sonal would return, Ma would again count her hair.

One day, when Sonal returned home after bathing in the lake, Ma sat her down and counted her hair—there was one golden hair missing! Ma was awfully worried. She frantically counted the hair again. The missing hair remained missing. She might as well have counted a hundred times, but what would be the use? If Sonal's hair started going missing like this each day, then how would

---

[1] A caste of bards and genealogists

one bear the loss? Ma was furious with Sonal. 'You aren't a child any longer, but your childishness has still not gone!' she screamed. 'Ultimately, only one's own common sense can be of use! I fuss so much, but you are just careless. You have gone and lost a hair worth a lakh. However much I scold you now, it won't help find the hair again. What is lost is lost. But be careful in the future. Dare you repeat this again! Then there will be no one worse than me!'

Sonal was mild-natured. Hearing Ma's harsh words, she began sobbing inconsolably. Ma's words had hurt her deeply. In her heart, she no longer wanted to be at home. And so, she sneaked out of her house. A little away from her home was a sandal tree. Sonal climbed on to it and sat on a branch. Hugging the tree close and weeping, she said in a pained voice:

'Climb, climb, re, sandal tree, climb high!'

As she sobbed, a tear from her eyes fell on the branch of the sandal tree. And at that very instant, the sandal tree began to grow taller and taller.

At home, when no one could find her, everybody began searching high and low for her. Searching-searching, they reached the sandal tree. There was Sonal, sitting on a branch! And the tree was still growing. Everyone craned their necks and peered upwards, and the tree kept growing—far beyond their reach.

It had now become rather difficult to get Sonal down. All her family members gathered at the base of the tree.

Soon, Sonal's girlfriends also joined in. They all began to wish with their hearts that the sandal tree would come down. But the tree didn't bend by even as much as a grain of rye. Ma began to shiver. Began wailing. Seeing Ma cry in this pitiful manner, Sonal's friends began to dance the *ghoomar*[1] and sing:

'Drums ring, *nagadas*[2] ring,
Her silver-like friends dance and sing,
Come down, Sonal Bai, O come down!'

Her friends tried a lot to pamper her, but stubborn Sonal would not relent. The drums rang and nagadas rang! And so loudly they rang! And again her friends danced! How much they danced! They begged her with folded hands, but it all fell on deaf ears. Sonal was unmoved. And every now and then, she would say to the sandalwood tree:

'Climb! Climb, re, sandal tree,
Climb high, re, climb high!'

And so, the sandalwood tree kept growing higher into the sky. From the ground below, Sonal now began to look like a little doll perched on its branch. This time, Ma sobbed:

'Drums ring, nagadas ring,
The daughter's mother does dance and sing,

---

[1] Traditional Rajasthani folk dance
[2] A percussion musical instrument, like a drum

Come down, Sonal Bai, O come down!'

But stubborn Sonal did not listen, not even to her mother. She sulked and said to the tree:

'Climb! Climb, re, sandal tree,

Climb high, re, climb high!'

Like the sun's rays that flash down to the earth from the skies, in the same way, the sandalwood tree began growing upwards from the eyes. Now from the ground below, Sonal looked like a small *chirmi*[1] flower. Her mother fainted and fell to the ground. This time, her father sang:

'Drums ring, nagadas ring,

The father does dance and sing,

Come down, Sonal Bai, O come down!'

But stubborn Sonal did not listen to even her father. Unmoved, she said:

'Climb! Climb, re, sandal tree,

Climb high, re, climb high!'

And so, the sandal tree kept climbing higher.

Perched on the branch, Sonal could now barely be seen from the ground below. Her father shouted her name and fainted, collapsing to the ground. But Sonal's heart didn't melt at all. Sitting on the branch, she could hear everything and see everything.

Sonal's little nephew was also present in the gathering. He saw the drama unfold and began aping everyone.

---

[1] The small red flower of a plant native to the desert

He began dancing and clapping. Then he began singing in his lisped voice:

'Drums ring, nagadas ring,
The face of the sun and the moon does dance and sing,
Come down, Sonal Bai, O come down!'

Now, Sonal was extremely fond of her nephew, who had a face as sweet as the sun and the moon. When she saw him dance and clap, her heart melted. She couldn't refuse the innocent child's request. Immediately, she said to the tree:

'Bend! Bend, re, sandal tree,
Bend down, re, bend down!'

No sooner did Sonal say this than the tree began bending to the ground. As if it were a shooting star from the skies. Within moments, it reached the ground! Her family was delighted. Her unconscious mother also quickly stood up. Wiping her eyes, she begged, 'My dear Sonal, I will never scold you again. Please forgive me a hundred times over.'

But deep within her heart, Sonal no longer felt any attachment to her family. She cared for no one except her nephew. Swiftly taking her nephew in her lap, she spoke to the sandalwood tree:

'Climb! Climb, re, sandal tree,
Climb high, re, climb high!'

It took Sonal a moment to say this, but it didn't take a moment for the sandalwood tree to shoot upwards into the sky. And so, the aunt and the nephew went high into the clouds, far beyond the sight of those on the ground.

Now what was to be done? Sonal's family begged her with folded hands, but Sonal had made up her mind not to listen. And so, she did not.

Both of them began to live on the tree itself. Every single day, Sonal's sister-in-law would get choorma in a box made of pure gold along with water in a pot made of pure gold. She would then sweetly implore Sonal to have the morning meal. There was no way Sonal could refuse her. As soon as her sister-in-law would come to the tree, Sonal would ask the tree to bend down. Within moments, the tree would come to the ground. Sonal would then swiftly take the choorma and the water and ask the tree to rise up. As soon as she would say the words, the tree would rise up into the sky as fast as rays of light. Sitting on the branch, Sonal would first feed her nephew choorma with great love and affection, and then have her share of the fill.

In this manner, many days passed by.

One day, a rajkanwar's[1] wedding procession halted below the sandalwood tree to rest for a bit. They were all hungry and thirsty. Sonal was moved at the sight of their parched lips and fallen faces. Her heart melted. So, from her box, she took a small morsel of choorma and dropped it to the ground.

---

[1] A prince

But as soon as that morsel touched the ground, it grew so large that even after all the people below ate to their heart's content, it wasn't finished. Then from her pot, she threw a drop of water on to the ground. Again, as soon as the drop touched the ground, it took the form of a pond of sweet water. All the members of the procession drank the cool and pure water.

After their thirst and hunger had been satiated, when the prince and other members of the procession began to wonder about this illusory delusion, they were left totally speechless. What magic had just transpired in front of their eyes? The rajkanwar couldn't digest this. He ordered his retainers to promptly climb up the tree and investigate this bizarreness! But when they climbed up the tree, they could find nothing. They looked under every branch and leaf but could see nothing anywhere. After they all admitted defeat, the rajkanwar himself decided to climb up the tree. He searched under every branch and every leaf. As he combed the tree, finally at the very top, between two leafy boughs, he sighted Sonal and her nephew.

When he saw the girl with hair of pure gold, he was stunned. He was even a little afraid. 'My Lady, who are you? A fairy of Inder,[1] an apchara[2] or a *daakan*[3]-demoness?' he asked.

---

[1] Indra, who is regarded as the king of the gods in Hindu mythology

[2] A nymph from heaven; apsara in Hindi

[3] A witch

Sonal replied softly, 'Neither am I a fairy of Inder. Nor am I an apsara from heaven. Nor am I a daakan-demoness. I am of a human body from the earth. I am upset with my mother, so I am hiding here. With me is my nephew.'

On hearing her sweet voice and on seeing her beauty and her gleaming hair of gold, the rajkanwar became infatuated with her that very instant. He lost his senses. In every leaf of the tree, he could see only Sonal's face. Caressing her hair, he said, 'I want to make you my queen. If you wish, come with me. Without you, there is no way I will go back to my kingdom even if I have to die. I will live out my days on this tree in your presence. Without you, I cannot live for even a moment.'

Hearing the rajkanwar, Sonal lowered her face and blushed. Softly, she said, 'I cannot leave my nephew behind. If you let me keep him with me all the time, then I might accept your offer.'

As soon as Sonal said this, the rajkanwar agreed. And so, Sonal agreed to the rajkanwar's proposal too. She sat in a golden chariot like a queen. Her nephew sat in her lap. She folded her hands, bowed her head and sought the blessings of the sandalwood tree and bid adieu.

The rajkanwar's kingdom was very far away from there. On the way, her nephew grew thirsty. His lips and throat felt parched. They came upon a large lake of pure and fresh water. Sonal asked her ladies-in-waiting to get some water for her nephew. But the ladies were hesitant. They told her that by drinking the water of this lake, a human would turn into a crow. 'But if you order, we will get it,' they echoed.

After hearing this, how could Sonal order so! She lovingly explained to her nephew that the water was bitter poison, and ahead was a lake of water as sweet as nectar—he could drink from that.

Soon a second lake came on their way. When Sonal asked the ladies-in-waiting to get water, they said that a human who drank the water of this lake would become a dog. 'But if you order, we will get the water,' they said again.

After hearing this, how could Sonal order so! Her nephew was dying of thirst, but what could she do? Wiping away tears, she said while kissing his cheek, 'Be a little patient. The water of this lake stinks. The next lake has water as sweet as milk.' She requested the rajkanwar to speed up the chariot, and it began to move at twice the speed.

Soon a third lake came on their way, brimming with water. Sonal said to her ladies-in-waiting, 'Now, hurry! Hurry!'

The ladies remained unmoved. 'Getting water won't take us a moment,' they said. 'Not like our feet will become sore! If you order, then why would we linger? But he who drinks the water of this lake will become a snake. Now we will do as you command.'

But how could Sonal command this? *A snake is worse than a crow or a dog*, she thought. It would be best to find the next lake. Without Sonal saying anything, the rajkanwar asked to have the chariot speed up. It began to gallop incredibly fast. Soon, they reached the fourth lake.

Nearly sobbing, Sonal cried, 'Run, ladies! Don't delay for a further second.'

But the ladies didn't move from their spots. Crestfallen, they said, 'Now we will do as you command. He who drinks water from this lake will become a peacock. We only await your orders. If you don't believe us, one of us will drink this water ourselves to prove our point.'

Sonal believed them fully, but what could she do? Her nephew was fainting; his eyes were swimming. Now his life would leave him, next second, his life would leave him! Sonal was stuck in a dilemma. If she made him drink the water, he would become a peacock. If not, he would surely die. The fifth lake was still far away. Better to become a peacock than die, she thought. If he lived, at least there was the chance that he could be turned back into his human form. But after death, nothing could be done. Now the small boy had only a few breaths left in him, for he had completely lost his consciousness. Even as she shed copious tears, she ordered, 'If he becomes a peacock, so be it! Run and get him water.'

The ladies-in-waiting now hurried to the lake. They fetched the water immediately and handed the pot to Sonal. As soon as the unconscious nephew was given a sip of water, he turned into a beautifully coloured peacock. He lowered his neck and called out: *Tuhooo. Tuhooo.* Sonal held him in her hands and wept. When the peacock saw his aunt cry in this manner, he too began to weep. They hugged each other and wept and wept. When they got tired of crying, the rajkanwar tried to convince Sonal to move on, but there was no way she would leave her nephew at the lake and go ahead. On the other hand, the rajkanwar was adamant that he would not take a step farther without Sonal. A complete deadlock it was.

Eventually, Sonal agreed to go with the rajkanwar, provided he would let her come to the lake every single day to feed her nephew. The rajkanwar agreed to this instantly. So Sonal hugged her nephew and bid him goodbye. As she left him behind, she sobbed and sobbed. The peacock followed her chariot for a while. Seeing this, Sonal wept even more. Ultimately, she fainted. Helpless, she left her beloved nephew behind with the other peacocks at the lake and fell unconscious in the lap of the rajkanwar.

After this, every single day, Sonal would take a box of choorma and a flask of *gangajal*[1] and go to the lake. Below the neem tree at the lake were separate-separate pots in which she would put the choorma and the water. She would feed her peacock-nephew with her own hands.

---

[1] Water from the River Ganges

Every day, as soon as he would see his dear aunt, the bird would fly to her. He would lie in her lap. After eating the choorma, he would joyously unfurl his beautiful feathers, dance and start calling out. She would chat with him for a long time. Shower him with love. Dance and play with him. But when she would leave for the palace, she would shed copious tears.

Some days passed in this manner.

At the palace, one of the rajkanwar's wives was jealous of Sonal. She hated the new queen's beauty and her hair of gold. The rajkanwar was besotted with Sonal and had stopped visiting the older wife. He spent every moment of the day in the intoxication of Sonal! The older wife was looking for ways to get even. Till now, no such chance had come her way. One day, she hatched a plan to get her revenge. The wife was convinced that this time she would succeed. She went to Sonal's chambers, and in a voice sweeter than jaggery, she said, 'My dearest sister, every day you go through the trouble of going to the lake. One day let me also have the chance to look after your nephew. I am really looking forward to seeing your handsome nephew.' 'This has been on my mind for many days, but I haven't been able to say it. If you allow it today, let me take the choorma and gangajal to the lake.'

Sonal thought these sweet words were indeed sweet. She agreed instantly. 'It is my good fortune that after so many days you have come here to meet me. Why did you wait for so long? My nephew is like your nephew. For such a trivial thing, how can I refuse? You may please do as you wish.'

Sonal then told her everything—how to recognize her nephew, in which land the lake was and where the pots were kept. The older queen kept nodding, but inside she was brimming with the poison of vengeance. She reached the lake without delay. Now Sonal's nephew was innocent like Sonal, and as soon as he heard her call, he came running. Excited, he spread his feathers and began to dance. But the older queen's heart was full of malice. She thought of neither the good nor the bad. Mad with rage, she grabbed the peacock's neck and twisted it. As soon as his neck was twisted, his feather umbrella collapsed and he fell where he was. The queen, without washing her hands, ate all the choorma and gulped all the gangajal. Then she returned to her palace with joy in her heart.

The next day, Sonal journeyed to the lake with food for her nephew. She ran hurriedly with excitement. It seemed to her that she hadn't seen her nephew for God knows how long. As soon as she reached the lake, she called out to him. Upon hearing her call, all the peacocks at the lake began wailing. She frantically looked everywhere for her nephew, but he was nowhere to be found. She called out again. In answer, the peacocks wailed even louder. Sonal's heart trembled as she thought of the possibilities. Half-crazed, she ran to every tree, looking and calling for her nephew.

Finally, below a tree she found the limp body of her nephew with a twisted neck and scattered feathers. All the peacocks gathered there. They stared at her and began wailing.

Maddened with grief, Sonal jumped towards the body and hugged it. The grief of her nephew's untimely death caused her such trauma that her own life left her. The peacocks wailed and wailed even more. The wind and the sky themselves began to weep.

The peacocks of the lake performed the last rites of Sonal and her beloved nephew. In grief, they all gave up food and drink. All day and all night they would wail and shed tears. In a few days, their lives left them. The lake dried up. All the trees and bushes also withered away.

Where Sonal and her nephew died there have now stood two worn-out sandal trees through many ages. They still grieve and wail for Sonal and her nephew.

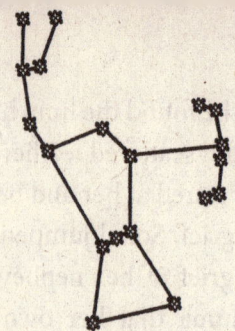

Aahedi, the Hunter

'There is a constellation of stars known as Aahedi [Orion, the Hunter]. In villages, stars are used by travellers at night to guide them along . . . It is clear that in observing and understanding the sky, people have divided stars into groups. Our calendars are constructed on the journey of the sun and the moon. The status of the stars is no less . . . '[1]

—Komal Kothari

[1] The months of the Vikram Samrat lunar calendar in Rajasthani are: starting with Baisakh, which coincides with April–May, followed by Jeth (Jyestha), Aasadh, Saavan (Shravana), Bhadua (Bhadra), Aasoj (Ashwin), Kati (Kartik), Mingsar (Margashira), Pou (Pausha), Mah (Magh), Phalgan (Phalguna) and Chait (Chaitra). The Hindi names are mentioned in brackets.

A beautiful spring night, pleasant beyond compare. In the jaggery-coloured night sky were encrusted countless priceless stars. Glimmering stars sparkled, as if a sorcerer had just swept the sky! The sweet songs of Phalgan from all four directions. *Loor* and *dhamaal*.[1] On a reed cot laid out in the courtyard, a grandson lay beside his grandmother. He kept insisting on a story every now and then. Gazing at every star with his innocent eyes, he said, 'Grandma, just yesterday you said you will tell me the story of Aahedi. Now why do you put it off? Why don't you tell me the story?'

'I will, my *laadal*[2] beta, I will! But let me at least hear the songs of Phalgan for a while! How sweet and how pleasing!'

The smart boy promptly caught on to his grandmother's mistake! Chuckling, he said, 'Sweet? Are these songs something to eat that they would be sweet!'

The grandmother spread a toothless smile and said, 'Beta, even the ears can tell bitter and sweet! When you grow up some more, you will understand these things.'

And saying this, the grandmother began seeing in the stars the memories of her lost childhood, her beauty and her youth! To wander in this manner across each star is no small pleasure!

---

[1] Loor and dhamaal are types of folk songs that are sung specially during spring.

[2] *Laadla* in Hindi, meaning 'dear'

The grandson again poked his dadi and said, 'Now the songs have stopped . . . I won't be able to sleep if you don't tell me the story of aahedi.'

The dokri wanted to wander many a star yet! So she found an excuse—'All these days, I've been teaching you about the *nakhtar*;[1] you first tell me their names and forms, only then will I tell you the story.'

'I remember all of those.'

'But tell me again, only then can we be sure!'

And in this excitement, he began rattling off the names of the constellations—'Chait . . . Saavan-Sarvan.'

The dadi laughed. 'After Chait comes Saavan? And you didn't describe the nakhtar of Chait at all!'

The boy laughed and began to stamp his feet, 'Oh I forgot, I forgot! The Chitra of Chait, with its mellow sparkle. The Baisakh Bicchu. Just like a scorpion. Legs in front and the stings at the back. The Bullocks of Jeth. Two harnessed bulls. A plough behind them. The Chaupad of Asadh. Four stars in four corners. The Panihari of Bhadua. As if a woman carries a pot on her head.'

'After Asadh comes Bhadua?'

'Why! Did I not already tell you about the constellation of Saavan? Saavan-Sarvan. With a stick across his shoulders like Sarvan.[2] Aasoj . . . Aasoj . . . '

---

[1] *Nakshatra* or 'constellation'

[2] Shravan from the story of Shravan Kumar in the Ramayana

Seeing her grandson get stuck, the grandmother said, 'The idhanis[1] of Aasoj. Two idhanis encrusted with invaluable pearls.'

The grandson made a face, 'Why do you interrupt me so? The *jhumka*[2] of Kati. A jhumka of small-small stars. The doe of Mingsar. Three large stars. Four dogs in four corners that do not leave the poor doe alone. The aahedi of Pou.' Saying this, the boy again insisted, '*Now* please tell me the story of aahedi.'

'There are still two nakhtars left.'

In a great hurry, the grandson said, 'The pair of Mah. Two-two gleaming stars in pairs. And the sickle of Phalgan. Twisted in front and straight at the back. Just like a sickle.'

The dadi asked one further question, 'When the Kirtya[3] moves to the right and beyond the moon, what happens?'

'Drought!' Saying this, the boy began to clap and laugh.

'Ni, beta, a drought is not a laughing matter,' interrupted the grandmother.

'Okay, I won't laugh now.' The boy sobered up.

'Okay, now listen to the story of aahedi carefully with open ears:

---

[1] Doughnut-shaped rests for balancing pots of water on one's head
[2] Umbrella-shaped earrings
[3] The constellation of Krittika, the third constellation of the twenty-seven mentioned in Hindu astrology

There was a doe. Very good and kind. True to her words. One day, after not drinking water for a long time, she felt extremely thirsty. And so she went, making *rammak-jhammak* sounds, to the waterfall.'

'Why rammak-jhammak? Of course she didn't wear anklets!'

'Beta, that doe was a *sati-suhagan*.[1] Why only anklets; she used to be laden with all kinds of jewels as married women are, all day long. Like wife, like husband. He never fought with her. And they had two sweet little children—just like you. Smart, well mannered and obedient!

Now, when the doe reached near the waterfall, there stood an aahedi, a hunter, with his bow and arrow drawn! Bare feet! A leather bag slung on his shoulders! Death in his glowering eyes! His eyes gleaming like embers! When she suddenly sighted the arrow, she started. But even then, she didn't run. She was very clever! To distract the aahedi, she smiled at him and said, 'Why do you stand with your arrow pointed at me . . . ?'

Such was the sorcery in her bewitching smile that the aahedi forgot to shoot the arrow and got lost in her words. 'What why! To kill you!'

---

[1] A married woman with a living husband

The sweet doe said, 'But I didn't come here to get killed. I came here to drink water! My throat is parched and I am dying of thirst. Let me first drink water at least!'

With the arrow still pointed at her, he said, 'And what if after drinking water, you trick me and run away, then?'

The doe smiled. 'Neither are you one to get tricked, and nor am I one to trick. This arrow of yours will not leave me! If you still doubt me, hold my ears and make me drink water!'

When he heard this, the aahedi began to believe the doe. The doe began to drink water from the gushing waterfall.

The hunter gazed at her as she drank. If his stomach wasn't aflame with this murderous hunger, one would not want to even look sternly at such an innocent creature! But this arrow was ready to rip into her soft body in an instant! This stomach is a sinner! Murderer!

After drinking her fill of water, the doe walked towards the aahedi with her tail wagging. She asked in an innocent voice, 'What will you get by killing me?'

Annoyed, the aahedi said, 'Surely not diamonds and pearls; only your meat, of course!'

The doe asked one further question. 'Am I not more beautiful living than as dead meat?'

'Of course you are beautiful, but beauty doesn't fill the stomach! My children have been hungry for three days! They must be wailing now!'

When she heard of the wailing children, her heart filled up. With moist eyes, she looked at the hunter's arrow and said, 'Hearing of your children's hunger, I am now helpless. Your children are like my children! How can I let them cry! But before I die, let me go and feed my milk to my children one last time. They must be waiting for me! Let me go and bid a final farewell to my husband too!'

Hearing these smart words from the doe, the aahedi could not stop himself from laughing. 'If I let an animal go after seeing it, it is a blemish on me. A blemish on the honour of my bow and arrow! I'm not so foolish as to fall into this trap!'

'But I am innocent and gentle. Really, I have heard of this talk of a trap for the first time. If I don't have the unfulfilled wish of seeing my husband and children one last time, then even as I die, I will bless you. I find your disbelief of my words worse than even death!'

Ram only knows how the hunter came to trust the doe's true words, but he happily allowed her to go to her home. The doe gratefully headed to her children. At home, she told them what had transpired at the waterfall. The crestfallen children gloomily heard the full story—up to the promise made to the aahedi. The doe was eager to return to the waiting hunter. And so, she asked her children to quickly drink her milk. However, both the kids declined point-blank.

They would not drink even a drop of her milk. When the doe asked the meaning of this, they said, 'Ma, where are you free now? You are bound by your promise, so your milk is also now pledged to the aahedi! We won't drink milk pledged to another!'

The doe had never thought that her little-little children would be so thoughtful! She was so happy to hear this! Then she took her children and went to her husband. Hearing of the promise made to the hunter, he said, 'The aahedi only cares about meat. I have a lot more meat than you! He will only be pleased to have me instead of you. You can then raise the children to be adults after me!'

But the doe was no less stubborn than her husband. And surely not foolish enough to walk into widowhood! Seeing both their parents walk into the fangs of death, the children joined them too. After all, on whom would they lean in the days of hardship? Who would raise them and look after them?

The hunter, counting every second to the return of the doe, saw four deer come towards him and was astounded! As soon as they came near, he glared at them and said, 'I knew you would betray me!'

Hearing this bizarre thing from the hunter's mouth, the doe asked, 'Why betray? Killing four will only mean more meat in your hands! Your children will love eating the tender meat of my children! I tried to stop them, but even then they have all come. If you don't believe me, ask them.'

The hunter shook his head. 'My foot I will ask! How can I kill your children for the sake of my children? You have kept your word like this. How can I shoot you!'

The doe argued, 'Your children must be wailing! At least take out the arrow from your quiver!

The hunter then forced himself to string the arrow on his bow. 'Just taking out the arrow won't be enough! Where is there strength in my arms any more . . . '

The grandmother wiped her moist eyes with her *odhna*[1] and said, 'Since that day all of them have been immortal. Poor death too wouldn't dare to as much as raise an eye at them! There, see the hunter? He's still ready to shoot with his arrow.'

The grandson kept gazing where his dadi's finger pointed. The dadi then began saying, 'And there stands the doe. Beside her, the husband, and behind them, their two little kids!'

The innocent child's eyes began to dance the ghoomar around those stars. In some time, the aahedi began to descend . . . Descending-descending, he landed on the child's hands! The child's soft fingers began playing with him!

---

[1] A drape worn over a ghaghra or lehenga, which is a traditional attire of women from the region.

Joo, Joo, Where Do You Go?

'. . . It feels to me like every letter of this story is a priceless gem . . . as if this story is about the collective subconscious of primal man. The subconscious mind of one human is different, and the collective subconscious is different. The subconscious of primitive man regards the non-living to be living like itself. Like them, stones, fodder and wood chat among themselves, smile and laugh and dance and play. Small and big creatures— lice, mosquitoes, ants, spiders, snakes, elephants, foxes and jackals—all wear clothes like men and women, deck out in jewels, bindis, tikkis and mehndi. Celebrate Holi, Diwali, Goga[1] and Teej. The trees, bushes and fruits and

---

[1] Gogaji is a folk deity worshipped across swathes of north-west India. Goga Navami is a festival celebrated in the lunar month of Bhadua (or Bhadra).

vegetables talk among themselves. Feel pleasure and pain. They see their reflections in nature. And feel like all of nature is their extended family. And behave with it as per this. Everything that man does, all the small and big creatures of nature also do. Sleep, eat, toil and dream.'

—Bijji

There was a joo.[1] She used to live on the head of a girl. The girl took great care of her. She would give her seera[2] and poori to eat. When the joo would walk on the girl's head, the joo would leave lines of gold and encrust her hair with diamonds and emeralds. The girl's head now had several lines of gold and was encrusted with priceless diamonds and emeralds. When the joo would consider leaving the girl's head and going away, her head would begin to itch. The girl would then quickly catch the insect and not let her leave her head. And if the joo didn't think of leaving, the girl's head would not itch at all!

One day, the joo decided to leave. She began to make her way very, very softly, but even then the girl's head began to itch. The girl got highly suspicious. To distract the joo, she began to ask her questions about this-and-that things—

_____

[1] Lice
[2] A sweet delicacy, like halwa

'Joo-joo, where do you go?'

'To pluck on chana leaves.'

'How do you pluck on them, ae?'

'*Bhachad-bhachad!*'

'How do you cut them, ae?'

'*Satak-satak!*'

'How do you cook them, ae?'

'With a *cham*!'

'How do you eat them, ae?'

'With a *sabad-sabad*!'

'And where do you sleep, ae?'

'Behind the stove.'

'What do you spread, ae?'

'The tray.'

'What do you cover yourself with, ae?'

'The sieve.'

'What do you keep under your head, ae?'

'The rolling board.'

'What do you keep under your feet, ae?'

'The rolling pin.'

'With what you do you keep warm, ae?'

'The blouse.'

'How do you cough, ae?'

'With a *khoo-khoo*!'

Then suddenly, the girl, catching the joo between her nails, said, 'You are *my* joo. Where do you go, ae?' But her nails had grown lately. The joo got crushed as soon as the girl pressed hard with her nails. The girl began crying. One teardrop fell on the crushed body of the joo, and instantly, it became a blood-red ruby. The girl sold the ruby for a lakh and a quarter. She celebrated her wedding with great *dhoom-dhaam* and enjoyed herself for many years.

The Joo's Curse

Once a joo got very upset and decided to travel to her nanire. Decked out in the sixteen adornments of women and the yellow glow of her gold ornaments, she set out. A vision of beauty. A woman, and all alone in this dense forest.

On the way, she met a seth. The seth was mesmerized by the joo's beauty and began to dream of living with her. He asked the joo, 'Joo-joo, where do you go?'

'To earn and fill my stomach,' said the joo.

The seth said, 'Why don't you stay at my home?'

'What will you feed me?' asked the joo.

The seth said, 'You will feast on jaggery! You will feast on sugar! You will feast on ghee!'

The joo sighed. 'I will get stuck in the jaggery, mixed in the sugar and solidified in the ghee. I won't stay with you.

You go your way; I will go mine.' Saying this, the beautiful joo went her way.

Going-going, she met a teli[1] on the way. The teli asked, 'Joo-joo, where do you go?'

'To earn and fill my stomach,' replied the joo.

The teli said, 'Why don't you stay at my home?'

'What will you feed me?' she asked.

The teli said, 'You will feast on crushed seeds! You will feast on oil! You will feast on oilcakes!'

The joo shook her head. 'I will get crushed with the seeds, I will drown in the oil and I will get buried under the oilcakes. So no, I won't stay with you. You go your way; I will go mine.' Saying this, the joo walked away.

Going-going, she met a mali[2] on the way. The mali asked, 'Joo-joo, where do you go?'

'To earn and fill my stomach,' said the joo.

'Why don't you stay at my home?' asked the mali.

Again, the joo asked, 'What will you feed me?'

'You will swing from trees to your heart's content! You will feast on rabdi![3] You will drink water from pots!'

The joo said, 'I will fall off the swing. I will get swept away while drinking water. So no, I won't stay with you. You go your way; I will go mine.'

---

[1] One who makes a living from extracting oil
[2] Gardener
[3] A dessert made from condensed milk

And so, she walked away. Going-going, she met a *moriya*.[1] Calling out to her, he said, 'Joo-joo, where do you go?'

'To earn and fill my stomach,' said the joo.

The peacock asked, 'Why don't you stay at my home?'

'What will you feed me?' the joo asked.

'I will get you grain! I will keep you in the moons of my feathers! I will light a crackling fire so that you can warm yourself as much as you want!' exclaimed the moriya.

It was winter. Bitterly cold. The idea of warming herself by a crackling fire appealed to the little joo. And so, she instantly agreed to the moriya's proposal. They both began living together. The peacock would get her grain to eat and she would warm herself by the fire. Both were happy and content.

But as fate would have it, one day, there was a terrible sandstorm. A great gust of wind blew in and the joo fell into the fire. Instantly, a blister formed. Scalded by the embers, she ran to the river to take a dip in the cool waters. But as soon as the water touched the giant blister, it burst with a pop! As the joo died, she cursed the river. And as soon as she cast the curse, the water of the river became as salty as salt.

---

[1] Peacock

The next day, a thirsty bull paused at the riverbank to quench his thirst. He took a sip but found the water like bitter poison. The bull asked the river, 'Just yesterday your water was like sweet nectar. Today it is like bitter poison; how come?'

The river replied, 'The peacock's broken home, the bitter Ganga and the hornless bull.' As soon as the river said this, the bull became hornless.

The bull passed a pipal tree. The tree asked, 'Just yesterday you had horns like javelins. How come you are hornless today?'

'The peacock's broken home, the bitter Ganga, the hornless bull and the trembling pipal.' As soon as the bull spoke, the pipal tree began trembling violently. Soon all its leaves fell off, and the pipal tree became as bare as a stick.

A dove flew to sit on the pipal tree. As soon as she came, she asked, 'Just yesterday you were lush and leafy; how come today you are as bare as a stick?'

The pipal tree replied, 'The peacock's broken home, the bitter Ganga, the hornless bull, the trembling pipal and the one-eyed dove.' Instantly, the dove became one-eyed and flew away. Ram knows who all were to be cursed this way!

Flying-flying, the dove came across a group of *paniharis*.[1] 'Just yesterday both your eyes were like ponds. How come you are one-eyed today?'

---

[1] Women who fetch water from a well or a pond, usually in earthen pots

The dove said, 'The peacock's broken home, the bitter Ganga, the hornless bull, the trembling pipal, the one-eyed dove and the dancing paniharis.'

As soon as the dove said this, the women began dancing all at once! On their heads were pots full of water, but they kept on dancing. The sound of so many dancing feet woke the King. He looked from the *jharokha*[1] and what a sight it was to behold! The paniharis with their pots of water! Going on dancing! Without pause! The King shouted, 'Why do you dance as if you are mad?'

Even as they danced, the women replied, 'The peacock's broken home, the bitter Ganga, the hornless bull, the trembling pipal, the one-eyed dove, the dancing paniharis and the pot-bellied king.'

As soon as this was said, the King's tummy inflated. It became hard for him to even move. All the queens saw the king's state and asked, 'Just yesterday your stomach was as flat as a pipal leaf; how did this happen?'

The king said, 'The peacock's broken home, the bitter Ganga, the hornless bull, the trembling pipal, the one-eyed dove, the dancing paniharis, the pot-bellied king and the buck-toothed queens.'

As soon as this was said, the teeth of all the queens grew as long their hands, as if they were witches. Their attendants

---

[1] An enclosed, overhanging balcony—a common feature in Rajasthani homes

wouldn't even want to come near them. Their female attendants fearfully asked their queens what had befallen them. Pat came the reply: 'The peacock's broken home, the bitter Ganga, the hornless bull, the trembling pipal, the one-eyed dove, the dancing paniharis, the pot-bellied king, the buck-toothed queens and the legless attendants.'

As soon as this was said, the women attendants became legless. They somehow managed to move with their hands. Seeing their state, the rajkanwar asked, 'Only yesterday you were all running about like horses; how come you are crippled today?'

The women attendants said, 'The peacock's broken home, the bitter Ganga, the hornless bull, the trembling pipal, the one-eyed dove, the dancing paniharis, the pot-bellied king, the buck-toothed queens, the legless attendants and the wailing rajkanwar.'

Instantly, the rajkanwar began weeping and wailing so much that he just wouldn't stop. He just howled away.

In this manner, the curse of the joo fell on everyone.

May Ram never let such curses befall even our enemies!

The Farming of Pearls

'I'll tell you a secret . . . A writer's own experience, craft, imagination and thought have a limit, but the stories heard from the mouths of men and women have neither a limit nor a boundary. Neither a limit to storylines nor to the collective thought processes. Neither a boundary to the imagination nor to experience.'

—Bijji

Stories, opium and wine—the older the better!

Ages ago, in the race of men, kings and kingdoms had just been created. Those days the breeze was a good one! The clouds were well regarded! The cycle of seasons would dance its ghoomar to the beats of merriment as per time! The rays of the sun and the moon would ask after the well-being of each person! The raja-rani would care for the happiness of their people before their own. If the happiness of every household was hard to ensure, then the raja would leave no stone unturned to take on their suffering! If in the chill of winter the people shivered in torn clothes, then the king would be shivering without clothes! If the people went hungry, he too would go hungry! He would think of others as he thought of himself. To fight enemies, the raja would take up arms along with his people. Otherwise, the people were banned from raising their swords. The raja would wander from house to house finding out the cause of people's pain. And if possible, the cause would be addressed instantly!

One day the raja of a certain raj set out to wander from village to village to inquire after the well-being of his people. Without awakening any attendants, he woke up two hours before dawn. He took his rani, went to the shed and harnessed the bullocks with his own hands. When the bullocks heard the click of a familiar voice, they set out. That Night of early Aasadh woke up to the sounds of the *ghunghroos*. Squinting her countless eyes, the Night saw the faces of the raja and the rani! No more worries now! Everything would be fine!

The king turned around, looked at his queen's face and said, 'Raina-de[1] greeted you. Why did you not greet her?'

The rani smiled. 'How could I make such a mistake? I greeted her before you did!'

When the king began to look at the sparkling stars, the rani said, 'How many times have I told you, but you think nothing of it . . . Why do you keep staring at Raina-de every now and then? She made this night so that the world can sleep! With her husband, the Sun God, she stays awake all night and sleeps all day. Staying awake each night is difficult, so as soon as she lies down, she closes her countless eyes and doesn't open them before evening. You men don't understand the nature of us women! We have to think of a thousand things!'

As soon as the rani ticked off the raja, he lowered his gaze. The bullocks went trudging along on their own. Gradually, Raina-de began to shut her eyes one by one. Free from the Sun God's arms, the enchantress was asleep on her bed while the Sun God got up and stepped out of their palace. In the east, he kept walking on the golden-pink path, as if vermillion were strewn on it. In all four directions, the ocean of light began to brim over! As soon as her man left, the Goddess of the Night shut all her eyes!

---

[1] Raina-de or Raina Devi is the Goddess of the Night, and her husband is the Sun God.

'Now you might as well look up,' the queen said to her husband. 'The door to the palace is shut and Raina-de sleeps alone!'

The raja turned around and looked. 'What is left to see now?' he said with a smile.

For a while his gaze met the rani's. 'How charismatic is Raina-de's husband's glowing, rotund face! After seeing his face, even we can see clearly!'

The rani was about to agree, when to her right she saw something quite bizarre in the fields. She could scarcely take another breath. The next instant, her eyes welled up. Pointing in that direction, she told the raja, 'Look carefully. I see a woman harnessed to a plough along with a bullock! And you are still called a king!'

The King turned. Indeed what the rani had said was true! Even while walking, how carefully she had observed! In this raj, never had he seen or heard something so bizarre! Every other fortnight, he would wander from village to village, but never had he seen such a spectacle. Then shame on his crown, his throne and his treasure!

The king stopped the carriage where it was and said in a choked voice, 'Till I return from there, you take care of the bullocks.'

Where was the time to say anything more than this? He hurried over in that direction. On the left side, an emaciated bull, and on the other side was harnessed a woman. A woman in mere name! A skeleton hung with withered skin!

Eyes buried in their sockets. Parched lips. Sweat caked with dirt. Panting after every footstep. And behind them, a man just as weak. A coarse cloth hung on his shoulders. Bare feet. Torn kurta. Tattered turban. Sowing fistfuls of bajri. With his swimming eyes, the raja could not tell whether the plough was moving forward or if the earth was moving backwards! One of the two surely, for the plough wasn't moving on its own!

Farmers who eat the toil of dust are also not as innocent as one thinks! The harder it is to fill one's stomach, the more devious one is. And on top of this, those who till the soil are the very personification of cunning! When he saw some high-born hurrying towards him, the farmer pointed his pitchfork at him and said roughly, 'Don't you come near! You'll frighten my bullocks! What? Is your treasure buried here?'

The raja took no offence at his roughness. But such harsh words had never reached his ears. Even then, despite his insides burning, he put a smile on his lips and said, 'Yes, my treasure is buried here. That's why I had to come here!'

Those warm words from the burning throat of the raja felt terribly bitter to the farmer! Even as he dragged the plough farther, he said, 'However smart you may be, use your smartness in your own home! Even if die, I won't leave these fields!'

The foolish farmer had taken offence. So the raja thought it would be best to get to the point straightaway.

He stepped slightly closer and said, 'Why have you harnessed a woman with the bullock?'

Clicking his tongue, the farmer replied, '*My* wife! And *I* have harnessed! What is it to you?'

The harnessed woman raised her eyes and looked at the raja. Then, panting, she moved forward with the bullock.

The King walked alongside. 'At least listen to me once.'

The farmer was quite insane. Poking the back of the bullocks with a sharp stick, he said, 'Two of my young sons have already died. What third thing is left to hear! Where do I have the time to listen to useless nonsense! All your life you've ordered servants around; now for what treasure have you come here? If you want to drink water, there is the pot, beside that babool tree.'

Hearing about the demise of the farmer's two young sons, the raja's heart was in his mouth. 'I did not come to drink water. I came here to help you.'

The farmer began shaking his head and asked his wife to move faster. 'No one helps anyone without some selfish motive! I won't even trust the clothes on my body! Leave me alone. I can be quite horrid!'

The raja tried to please him, 'You aren't horrid at all. Pain and suffering have riled your heart! I'm ready to give you one bullock from my carriage. Release your wife at once.'

Now the farmer understood his selfish motive. As soon as he was asked to release his wife, every pore of his body flared up. Grinding his teeth, he said, 'Give my wife in exchange for a bullock? I'm not such a fool. Get lost as you came, else no one will be worse than me! You see a weak person and think you can take me on? Even if two people like you come here, I wouldn't be scared!'

The raja began to think that it must have been the unbearable grief that had made this man's heart totally twisted! He must doubt even the wind and the rain! He must think that even the sun rises for its own self-interest! The fault was entirely of poverty and tragedy. The King now folded his hands. 'My wife is sitting in the carriage. To me, even the apcharas[1] of Inder Lok appear unattractive in front of her. If you are suspicious, then I will remain standing here. You can send your wife there and get a bullock. Seeing her suffering like this, my heart bursts!'

The farmer swung his pitchfork at the King and said, 'And all this time, my plough will stand idle? Fool! Only the pearls sowed on time bear fruit! You don't seem to have ever farmed the land!'

Seeing his reeling wife, the raja thought to cut the empty talk. He said, 'I won't waste even a second of yours. In the time it takes for the bull to come here, I am ready to get harnessed in place of her!'

Hearing this, the farmer was somewhat pleased. He tried to smile, but there was no place in that skeleton for

---

[1] Apsara in Hindi, meaning 'a celestial nymph'

something as useless as laughter! He softened somewhat and said, 'Yes, this time you have spoken sense. But if your wife refuses, then?'

'No chance she will refuse. And even if she does, till your work is done I won't leave your plough!' the raja said, placing the log on his shoulder.

The farmer was not able to understand the meaning of this unsolicited goodness. Spitting at the king to ward off the evil eye, he said, 'You, brother, are some madman it seems! This sort of goodness, who can afford? Still, there is no bigger sin than being good to another—always remember these words of mine.'

Even as he pulled the plough with the bull, the raja said in astonishment, 'Sin?'

'Yes, sin! What do you even know yet? Maybe that's why you are feeling proud of your goodness!'

The raja was not able to understand the farmer's riddles. But the raja cared only for his own understanding. After all, why entangle in the web of another's understanding? What puts the heart at peace is the best! Let the farmer worry about his own heart. Even then, the questions in the raja's heart had not fully died out. He quietly kept pulling the plough.

Back at the carriage, when the rani saw the spectacle of the woman standing in front of her, she could scarcely believe her eyes. Who knows in hope of what happiness she had continued to live for so many years and still wanted to live! *It's not a hallucination, is it?* The rani rubbed her eyes and looked at the panting woman. Then the woman spoke slowly in a soft voice, 'Your man asks to send a bullock there.'

Sense returned to the queen like a flash of lightning. As soon as she heard the woman's words, she understood everything. She said, 'One bullock won't be enough. Both will have to be taken. Your bull won't be able to manage with this one!'

As she got off to free the bulls, the rani asked, 'But the plough still moves! Who pulls it in your place?'

The woman replied softly, 'Your husband . . .'

The rani already suspected this. But as soon as it was confirmed by the woman, it was as if a fiery dagger pierced her heart! In a choked voice, she said, 'I'm heading there. You get both the bulls!'

Saying this, she rushed from there. She hurried to the field and quickly began untying the sickly bull. 'I should have taken the place of the woman! How could you have done this injustice? Now I too must pull the plough with you.'

The farmer kept staring as the rani harnessed herself along with the raja and began pulling the plough. Now he did not need to goad anyone along! The raja-rani were pulling the plough on their own!

When the farmer's wife arrived with the two bulls, the farmer spoke up. 'The bulls are here. Now stop.'

'Let us finish this line at least,' said the King as he pulled the plough.

The farmer argued no more. Just quietly kept on putting bajri seeds through the funnel on the plough.

Reaching the edge of the fields, the raja and rani stopped on their own. The farmer began to harness the bulls in their place. As he was doing this, Ram knows what occurred to him that he began to look at the raja with surprise. 'I have mulled and mulled, but I'm tired of thinking for what end did you go to such lengths?'

Hearing these strange words from the farmer's mouth, the raja-rani were left speechless. No easy answer occurred to anyone. After a while, the rani tried, 'Can one person not help another without any selfish interest?'

What was there to even think about in this! The farmer immediately shook his head. 'No.'

Then the raja thought that maybe if he told the farmer everything, he might find it all more believable. So he smiled at the farmer's doubt and said, 'I am the raja of this land, and she is my rani! To destroy the suffering of each person—this is my only self-interest!'

The raja wanted to go on, but when the farmer interrupted, he stopped. Shaking his head, the farmer said, 'This self-interest is surely the biggest! Make me king and I would also be ready to have myself harnessed in the plough of some farmer! What is the big deal in this! To be a king is no small thing. He is thought to be an incarnation of God. Now you go your way. I understand everything now!'

After this, the raja-rani left their carriage there with the bulls and left on foot.

When the time came and the clouds poured forth, the farmer's bajri grew as the farmer wished. Pods that were two-two feet long. Encrusted with shining grains! But a matter of extraordinary surprise—that in the line where the raja-rani pulled the plough, instead of bajri, invaluable pearls began to shine! But the poor farmer had not seen pearls, even in his dreams. Then how could he tell that they were pearls! Thinking them to be pebbles, he tied them into a separate cloth and went straight to the Raj Durbar.

The raja recognized the farmer as soon as he saw him. When the raja respectfully asked him if he had been fine, the farmer replied with his characteristic dourness, 'Did I not tell you that helping another is the biggest sin!'

The raja asked in surprise, 'Why, what has happened?'

'What else could have happened? The rows you ploughed, these shining pebbles have grown there! Neither can one chew them nor can one grind them . . . !'

Telling the raja off to his face, the farmer opened the cloth and looked at the raja. 'Your goodness has sprouted forth this fruit! The rest of the field was saved; that was luck! Else I would have suffered badly.'

The king began laughing at the man's innocence. 'Silly! These are invaluable pearls! *Pearls!* Did you not say then that the pearls sowed on time bear fruit? These are those pearls! Can you not tell pearls at all?'

The farmer replied morosely, 'When have I ever seen damned pearls? I only knew the saying, so I blurted it out that day. But these pearls don't fill the stomach, do they? I'd rather you weigh me as much grain.'

The king again laughed at the poor man's innocence. Then he patiently explained, 'Where does one even find such invaluable pearls! One pearl would be more than enough to fill the stomach of seven of your generations! Together, they'd be more than enough for the kingdom! But these pearls have grown in your fields, so how can I take them? You keep all of them!'

The farmer shook his head. 'No, no. No chance that I'll keep them! Without toiling, won't I become lazy? I don't like not to toil even for a second! These pearls befit you! Now it's up to you and your pearls. My small contribution to the treasury of the raj!'

Staring at this brainless farmer, the raja said, 'Your small contribution will do good for the kingdom . . .'

As soon as he heard of goodness, the farmer flared up again. Annoyed, he said, 'If you want to do good for the kingdom, then go on doing good till you are fed up! But always remember my words: there is no greater sin than goodness for another!'

'You still think this?'

'Yes, I do! I don't take anything given to me. My wish!'

'But how did such a wish come about?'

'This I myself don't know. What can I say!' Saying this, the farmer returned as he came. The raja kept calling after him, but the farmer cared nothing for it!

The Kelu Tree

'Heard this story from Santokh Kanwar. Parental home Borunda. Caste Charan. She heard this story in her marital home, Devariya, from a barber's wife. Twenty-four years old.'

—Bijji

At the hour of death, the parents impressed upon their seven sons many a time to keep their only sister well, to take good care of her and not to let her suffer in any way. To find her a good match. Give her a good dowry. If she suffered after they went, even after dying they would not attain *moksa*.[1] However, the son's wives were absolutely horrid. If they had their way, the sister would suffer for sure.

---

[1] Moksha in Hindi, meaning 'salvation'

The brothers reluctantly agreed to their parents' wishes, but the old couple could not trust them much. Their lives left their bodies with great difficulty.

And with the death of the parents, the wives lost whatever shame they had left. They would make their nanad[1] toil all day. They would curse and abuse her. The nanad would go behind the house and sob to lighten her heart. Every day, the wives would mutter and curse that the man who married the girl would surely have rotten karma; so useless she was! However, the nanad was actually quite deft and thoughtful. Beautiful too. If her sisters-in-law didn't see this, what was she to do!

It was the colourful festival of the Teej of Saavan, to welcome the monsoon. On every tree, swings were hung. In every lane, groups of girls, decked out in their finery and *singaar*,[2] appeared. But that poor girl, the sister to seven brothers, stood crying behind her house in filthy clothes. With whom could she share her pain!

When the youngest brother saw his sister sobbing, his heart melted. In all the other homes, today was the day when sisters would deck out in their best. The brother slowly approached his sister and asked her the reason of her misery. However, she kept silent.

---

[1] Husband's sister

[2] *Shringaar* in Hindi, meaning 'women's make-up and finery'

Though the youngest brother was scared of his wife, he still had some respect and love for his sister. With some trouble, he had found a prospect for his sister and had fixed up the engagement. She was to be married on the fifth day of Saavan—just two days hence! The sister would go away to her husband's home. Ram knows when she would return!

When the brother kept asking questions, the sister finally revealed to her brother her pain: she too wanted to wear a beautiful new ghaghra and *chunari*[1] and go play and celebrate on the swings. The brother went to all his sisters-in-law to ask them to lend their fine clothes, but none of them agreed. He finally went to his own wife. She agreed but on one condition: if her silken chunari or ghaghra were spoiled, she would dye them again in his sister's blood! The brother thought what damage could come in just one day. Even then he asked his sister to be extremely careful and handed her the new clothes. And got bound by the promise he made to his wife.

The sister's luck was so bad that as she swung on the swings, it suddenly began to pour so heavily that despite her being most careful, the silken clothes got drenched. Fully soaked! The colour of the chunari began to run. In great fear she went home. As soon as her brother's wife saw the state of the clothes, she flared up and hissed like a black snake! Went and lay down. The husband tried to calm her,

---

[1] A tie-dyed drape

but she just would not listen. 'Being a man, you go back on your words,' she taunted. 'Either spit seven times and lick it up or fulfil your promise.'

One can live without a sister, but how can one live without a wife! Till his sister was killed and the chunari was not dyed in her blood, the brother's wife vowed that she would partake neither grain nor water. Fast unto death! The brother said that the day after tomorrow the groom would arrive with the wedding procession. Who all would he give answers to? To which the wife replied, 'If a witch runs away before her wedding, what can her brothers possibly do? Not a soul would get to know what happened.'

Helpless, the brother had to agree. At midnight, as the girl lay sleeping, the two cut her head off. After dyeing the chunari in her blood, the wife broke her fast and gorged on choorma to her heart's content! The brother took his sister's body two miles away, dug a deep pit and buried it. With an hour of the night left, he came back and quietly went to sleep.

Where the sister was buried, there began to grow a tall and slender kelu[1] tree, which swayed gently in the breeze. As fate would have it, the girl's *jaan*[2] procession came

---

[1] Deodar

[2] Also known as *baraat*; 'the wedding procession of the groom'

down that same road. Suddenly, the groom's father saw the tall, slender tree swaying in the breeze. He thought how great it would be to tie the *toran*[1] at the bride's home! He asked the barber in the procession to go and cut the tree and get it.

But what a matter of surprise it was that when the barber bent down to cut the tree and a voice from the ground was heard:

'Barberji, O Barberji, don't cut this kelu tree.
Sinner is the brother, sinner his wife.
Dyed the chunari with the sister's life!'

The barber fled in fright. Panting, he returned and narrated the tale. The groom's father said that surely he must have imagined it. He then ordered the *dholi*[2] to cut the tree.

The dholi hurried and bent to cut the tree, when, just as before, he heard:

'Dholiji, O Dholiji, don't cut this kelu tree.
Sinner is the brother, sinner his wife.
Dyed the chunari with the sister's life!'

---

[1] A talismanic wooden door hanging made of a tall, slender trunk, which is tied by the groom at the bride's doorway as part of wedding rituals
[2] Drummer

The dholi also fled in fright. Then the groom's younger brother gathered courage and came. He too was just about to cut the tree, when he heard a voice:

'Devarji,[1] O Devarji, don't cut this kelu tree.
Sinner is the brother, sinner his wife.
Dyed the chunari with the sister's life!'

And the younger brother fled in fright. The groom's elder brother mocked all of them and said, 'Go and die in a puddle of water. A five-year-old kid isn't as scared as you all are.' Muttering, he headed to the tree. He was just about to cut the tree, when he heard:

'Jethji,[2] O Jethji, don't cut this kelu tree.
Sinner is the brother, sinner his wife.
Dyed the chunari with the sister's life!'

The older brother also took to his heels. Told his father everything. The father got quite annoyed. He said, 'You all are just wasting time. Can't cut a little tree, how will you even sire children?'

---

[1] Husband's younger brother
[2] Husband's older brother

He walked towards the tree. He held it with his right hand and was just about to cut it with his axe, when he heard a voice from the roots:

'Susraji,[1] O Susraji, don't cut this kelu tree.
Sinner is the brother, sinner his wife.
Dyed the chunari with the sister's life!'

The father of the groom was scared. But he thought maybe he was imagining things, so he once again got ready to use his axe. Again the same voice called out to him, and this time even he fled! 'Brothers, it was true! Never seen such a thing, never heard such a thing!' he huffed.

This time, the groom went himself. As soon as he held the tree, he heard:

'Husbandji, O Husbandji, you may cut this kelu tree.
Sinner is the brother, sinner his wife.
Dyed the chunari with the sister's life!'

The soft stem got hacked in one blow of the axe. But yet another wondrous thing happened—as soon as the tree was chopped off, the earth miraculously parted and from it emerged a beautiful woman, her face veiled!

---

[1] Father-in-law

Then she kept no secrets from her husband. Told him all that had befallen her. Hearing everything, the wedding procession did not even go to the village. They took their wedding *feras* around the stump of the kelu tree instead of the holy fire! And the jaan took the *beendni*[1] and returned from there itself . . . !

The sister of seven brothers had a wonderful life in her marital home. Bathed in milk and gave birth to healthy children! And as for those seven brothers and their wives, they got struck by the plague. Such a death!

---

[1] Wife

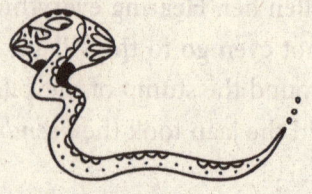

Naagan, May Your Line Prosper

'I am stunned after reading 'Naagan Thaaro Bans Badhe' [the original story title] . . . The form of this story of yours is like a problem in mathematics. In mathematics, problems don't have an answer, they have a solution . . .'

—Mani Kaul, director of *Duvidha*

The tale of a tale.
The mischief of mischief.
There were three villages.
Two abandoned, and one, never settled only.
In which lived three potters.
Two fools, and one knew not about making pots only.
In which were boiled three grains of rice.
Two raw, and one did not get boiled only.
For which were welcomed three pandits.

Two on a fast, and one would not eat only.
Who were gifted three cows.
Two sick, and one would not give birth only.
Who birthed three calves.
Two lazy, and one would not move only.
Who were sold for three coins.
Two fake, and one not in use only.
Which were tested by three sonars.[1]
Two blind by night, and one can't see by day only.
Who were dealt three smacks.
Two missed, and one did not hit only.
The sonars ran to drown in the wells.
Two dry, and one had not water only.

So may Ramji bless us all—that in this world of men, the rich are worshipped for their wealth, kings are respected for their thrones, warriors honoured for their valour, the strong known for their strength, poets and craftsmen famed for the finesse of their art, but Viliyo, the barber, was widely loved throughout the land for his brains. It seemed as if from every pore of his body seeped knowledge instead of sweat. A large head, sharp nose, thick eyebrows that met in the middle, a moustache as black as ink, wavy hair, long arms, shapely white teeth that gleamed like pearls and a voice so pleasant that when Viliyo spoke, it felt like

---

[1] Goldsmith

flowers were being showered. He could explain anything and everything he was asked. Everyone would bow to him, and people would fall over each other to take him with the wedding jaan. He nurtured deep bonds with all. No bad habits. Well meaning. Loving. A fount of the wisdom of old stories.

One evening, when he was lying down on a cot after supper, going *gud-gud* on his hookah, his wife said, 'After a full twenty-one nights you returned just yesterday, and yet you have said yes to be a part of the wedding procession of choudhary[1] baba's son! That too at dawn tomorrow! Even guests at our home spend more time here than you! All day all three children keep chanting *jisa-jisa*[2] and you don't care at all. Respect for others has a boundary too . . . Anyone comes along and you say yes to them!'

Viliyo smiled, looked at his wife's face and said, '*Bawali*,[3] even to death, I won't say no. I will accept her invite with a smile and open arms, the same way. I have sworn an oath to never say no . . . it won't be—'

Interrupting her husband, she said, 'To the woman of your house and your children you sure know how to say no. And you take pride in your oath *not* to say no!'

---

[1] A form of address for a male of the jaat caste
[2] A term of respect for father or father figure
[3] Silly

He caught her hand and made her sit beside him. Viliyo kept the hookah pipe aside. 'In this mischief, none can match you! Are you and the children separate from me? We are all one soul. Our bodies are separate, so what? Bawali, one says no to others, but how can one say no to oneself? Tell me, is it only when I tear my heart out and show you that you will know what's in my heart?'

'I know everything . . . Nothing in your heart is hidden from me,' she replied. 'But if you know my heart at all, then tell me—in distant lands, do you ever miss me?'

Playing with his wife's wrist, Viliyo replied, 'But you and I are one . . . Who would I miss and why would I miss?'

Trying hard not to smile, she said, 'With your words you can even defeat God, then what am I! But a house only lights up with the presence of the man! If the sun doesn't rise in the sky, how would the earth light up? All these empty words don't make up for the missing sun.'

'You have spoken like the true match of Viliyo barber. You are right; if the Devi of Fate herself comes and clashes with me, I can for once put her in her place . . . Listening to my stories, the entire world swoons. Everyone sings my praises. I'm rather tired of hearing them. But it is only now that I have understood the real meaning of things. Stories are just tricks of the tongue! Beauties of the lips! But the secrets of the heart are unseen! Invisible! There is no connect between the heart and the voice. The heart's essence is in its silence. All these people . . . We have grown up together since we were children, so I can't avoid speaking to them. And then years of storytelling have made me addicted. I can leave this blabbering as easily as I can leave the hookah. I think that even after I die if someone asks me the meaning of something, I'll have to speak! Truly, I don't care about fame at all. But you tell me, if I refuse people, would they understand? In their arguments, the moment they get entangled, they come straight to me! Every person looks at my face with hope; in that moment does it do to avoid them? The jeev that is born must go one day. Many a day has rolled past; only a few are left! Why hurt someone by saying no!'

Smiling and sulking at the same time, she said, 'All of us at home are there to be hurt . . . We won't let anyone else's turn come at all. So don't you worry about this!'

'I am being honest. With you around, I worry about nothing at all.'

The next day at dawn, when Viliyo left to join the village-choudhary's son's wedding procession, his wife came to see him off at the border of the village. A sweet breeze was blowing. Such a pleasing visage of the darkness had never been seen before. Its touch made an endless glow stir in their hearts. The light of every star seemed to grow in their eyes a quarter more. Viliyo turned and looked back at his wife three–four times. Despite the sea of darkness separating them, her face seemed to glimmer like the moon.

At the home of the village-choudhary, all the other guests were waiting for Viliyo. He reached there right on time. Viliyo held a hookah in one hand. A stick encrusted with silver sequins tucked under his arm, a cloth on one shoulder and a scarlet bag slung on the other. After greeting him, the choudhary said, 'Viliyo, you will surely live long. We just mentioned your name and you emerged with your hookah as if you were hiding here itself!'

Twenty-one carriages were harnessed and ready. Once Viliyo had reached, everyone settled down and soon the bulls started to move. The sound of the bells around their necks rang out in the air.

The bulls kept moving forward. The jaan stopped after twenty-four miles by the side of a lake. They gave the bulls water to drink and then paused to rest in the cool shade of a huge, leafy banyan tree. The choudhary said, 'We will move again only after eating our meal. I will go and get some flour, ghee, dal, masala and return soon.' Nearby was a large town. To arrange for dal baati,[1] the choudhary left for the town with a bag on his shoulder.

---

[1] A Rajathani delicacy comprising wheat dumplings crushed and served with ghee, jaggery and dal

The choudhary was getting his purchase weighed at a shop owned by a *baniya*,[1] when he saw the strangest sight—so strange that he could not stop staring. A lad of the baniya's household—extraordinarily handsome—had a living *naagan*[2] coiled around his neck! Jet black and as long as two men! But strangely, there was no fear to be seen, neither in that lad nor in anyone else. He was feeding her saffron milk with a golden spoon. And making her smell rose, *champa* and *kewra* flowers.

Surely, Viliyo can explain this! He bought all he needed and hurried back. When he returned to the camp, he handed all the things to another barber to cook and quickly sat beside Viliyo. Who could possibly be patient after seeing such a strange sight! He said, 'Today you will be exposed. If you can't explain this sight, I will take back all the sweets and gold chains, Viliyo. If you can explain, then with this chain of pure gold I will also give you a flower made of five gold mohurs.'

The choudhary then explained to Viliyo what he saw in full detail. When Viliyo said nothing, the choudhary said, 'You can't beguile us by blowing smoke from your hookah. Today if you cannot give answers, you need to hold your ears with your hands and admit defeat. Only then will I rest.'

---

[1] Man from the traders' caste
[2] Also written as *naagin*, meaning 'female snake'

'If you are having second thoughts about the gold chains and sweets you gave me, so be it,' said Viliyo. 'But this tale is an extraordinary one! Let everyone gather around so that they too can partake in the pleasure. Choudhary baba, is this a yawn that you will have it alone?'

And so, everyone gathered and sat down. And thus began Viliyo:

'The young man who feeds the naagan saffron milk with a golden spoon is the only son of the richest seth of that village. Today the seth-sethani have crossed sixty. Of course they haven't been sixty since they were born. They crawled and then stood up on their legs. Their childhood passed by. They were engaged and then married. He was fifteen that time; she was eleven. Three years later, she left her parents' home and started to live with him. One year passed . . . Five years passed . . . And soon, in this manner, twenty-five years had passed, but the sethani's womb could not conceive a child. Strands of white started to appear on the seth's head but no son yet. There was no measure to the amount of wealth in his haveli. When the treasury of the raj was depleted, it was the seth who would save its honour. His seat was beside the king himself. He had endless wealth and boundless power. But the jibes at his childlessness pierced his heart like a dagger. The sethani was still stoic, but the seth's restlessness never diminished for even a second. Inside, he was being eaten away. When his wife saw him restless and worried, she too was saddened. She would tell him that what use is it to fret about something beyond one's control? Why fume in vain? In death, neither son, nor grandson nor daughter-in-law would go with them.

The seth would sigh deeply and say, "Only I know the pain in my heart. You don't. I am the seth who sits on a throne beside the king's, and people don't want to see my face in the mornings for fear of it being an ill omen! When people turn around and spit to ward off bad luck after looking at me, I want to jump into a well! After we're gone, our family name will be forgotten. What is the meaning of this wealth if there is no one to guard it? In homes where there are not even enough morsels to eat, children abound! But here! It seems God has forsaken us! I force myself to go about my business, but my heart is not in it at all."

On people's suggestions, the seth tried many tricks and spells, burnt up a lot of his wealth, but it made no difference at all. The glimmer of diamonds and pearls did not light up the darkness of the sethani's womb.

One day, it crossed all limits. A farmer was going to his fields to celebrate the festival of Akha Teej[1] to

---

[1] The festival of Akshaya Tritiya

bring good luck. However, his path crossed with the seth. The farmer didn't even greet the seth. He just spat thrice[1] and did an about-turn. No reverence for the seth, no respect for his wealth! The seth was stunned. His feet would not move. The world closed in on him. He held his head and slumped down on the ground where he was standing. *What use is such a life! What use is such maya![2] This day was all that was left to see!* His head began to swim, and the earth around seemed to heave. He blacked out and collapsed.

When people began coming and going to the markets, they found the seth lying unconscious on the dusty ground. They fanned him, sprinkled cool water in his eyes. Then when the seth's eyes half opened, they quickly carried him to his haveli. As the sethani fanned him, gasping and spluttering he told the sethani what was in his heart. His every word felt like a scorching ember against her heart. Hot tears came to her eyes. That day, even the sethani's patience gave way. How could she bear to see her husband suffer so! It was not possible to trick her womb, but she would have to find some or the other way to trick her husband. Without taking anyone's advice, she hatched a plan.

---

[1] In some cultures, spitting is believed to ward off an ill omen.
[2] Wealth or splendour

After some time, pressing her husband's head, she said, "Don't make yourself suffer like this. I will use a *mantar*.[1] Nine months hence, if this haveli doesn't ring with the sound of clanging *thaals*[2] to announce the arrival of a child, you might as well never believe me ever again. Now, this suffering will only endanger the effect of the mantar. Promise me that you will not be pained or upset in this manner, ever!"

The man tried to smile. "If what you say turns out to be true, I would smile all day!"

"Only the glimmer of the smile on your lips will light up my womb," she replied.

Whence the seth began smiling so much that even without a reason, he would always have a smile on his lips.

She revealed her plan to a trustworthy *naayan*.[3] Handing her a bag of a hundred gold mohurs, she said, "See, besides the two of us, even God should not get to know about this plan."

But the naayan was a good woman. Returning the bag of mohurs, she said, "This is my home. I will ask for this if and when I have to go to any lengths.

[1] Mantra

[2] A ritual where the birth of a child is announced by beating bronze thaals, or plates, in the doorways and lanes

[3] Barber's wife or nurse. The barber and his wife are usually retainers to upper-caste families.

Till then, let this lie in trust with you. Now I will take these mohurs only once this plan of yours actually comes true. If there is truth in a mother's heart, a child can be conceived outside the womb as well! One and a quarter times better than one born from one's own womb!"

The sethani said as she touched the naayan's chin, "Jaggery for your tongue! To prove the truth in the mother's heart, I will create a new womb. This truth will not be born of the womb I have been fated by the Devi of Fate! This will be a different womb! I will create this womb!"

The seth continued to smile in the same manner. After seven days or so, the naayan came running to the seth and said, "I won't settle for a reward less than a necklace! The sethani is expecting! Nine months to this date, you will hear the sound of a baby in this haveli!"

Unbounded happiness left the seth speechless. He began gaping at the naayan in a manner as if he held the baby in his hands that very minute. Then he said, "Even a *navlakha*[1] necklace would be too little!"

Beaming, the naayan replied, "When we poor have cravings we make do with *maith*,[2] coal and chalk. But when the sethani has cravings, they won't be calmed

---

[1] Necklace worth nine lakhs
[2] Fuller's earth or *multani mitti*

with such things. Send for berries, dates and raisins! Nimbu achaar, malpua,[1] sweets and amchoor[2] we can make at home—no need to worry about those."

The seth said, "No, no, no amchoor-famchoor. In case it upsets the stomach!"

The naayan continued to smile from behind her veil. "You men won't understand these things. A woman's life is tough to live out. This garbage of wealth and maya doesn't really ease it. One has to have sour and spicy things—buttermilk with chillies! When one wants to have maith, almonds and pistas are like stones. Chalk can taste sweeter even than dried fruits!"

"Then no need to ask me. Do as you think right. Whatever you ask me to get, I will fill the stores with it."

The naayan left. How could the seth be patient that day! *Dham-dham* he climbed up the stairs and went to the sethani. The happiness in his eyes and the excitement in his voice were limitless. He began saying, "Even God cannot measure my happiness today. If I had to give up all my maya to become a father, I would not have refused. There are things in this world bigger than maya; this I have understood fully well today. I will give you a navlakha necklace as a gift. A navlakha necklace!"

---

[1] Fried pancakes soaked in sugar syrup
[2] Dried raw mango

Then after pausing for a while, he continued, "What caution can *I* advise! It will be your caution and care that will make this life worthwhile. As much care as I take of myself, what would it matter! Don't listen to what these illiterates say and end up eating something strange. These people can digest stones also, but we are different! If you have sour buttermilk with chillies, it will sting our baby. Have control over yourself! Also, why did you hide this from me? You should have given me this news first. Now let's see how well you take care of yourself!"

What could the sethani have said? She stood there quietly. It was as if the seth's words were on wings! Unembarrassed, he asked, "How many days has it been? It was checked properly, no? I never heard you throw up! I hope it doesn't turn out that—"

"Why eat your head about what you don't know?" his wife interrupted. "Don't say these silly things in front of others. No one will say anything to you; they will sing praises about my brains!"

"Why? What is there to sing praises about? The whole world has birthed and birthed till they are all tired. But we never sang praises of anyone!"

That day onwards the seth closed all his accounts. In his books, he stuck calendars and astrological charts and began to make calculations every day. He would think to himself: *One hour has passed, now two . . .*

Now it is evening, now it is dawn. Here is yet another golden sunrise. This lazy sun moves across the sky so slowly. Has dragged himself to midday finally. Hope he hasn't stopped at midday! This sun doesn't budge! Will this pitch dark night pass by? What if the sun forgets to rise for two fortnights! If only someone can shorten the days, I will hand him all this wealth! Ram knows when these nine months will pass! Nine months for the poor, nine months for the rich! How is this fair? This God is also pot-headed! Silly!

Every day at sunrise, he would look intently at the sethani's stomach. *Where . . . where . . . ?* Today the stomach hasn't risen! Still as deflated as the drum of a luckless man!

After what seemed like many ages, seven months passed by! The seth thought that now the stomach had risen somewhat. But now how will these two months pass? Till now, nature had not floundered. But who would take responsibility for the remaining two months? Every now and then, he would ask the sethani if she was in pain, and ten times a day, he would ask her to be patient. After all, how many days were left? "Bear a little bit more . . . some more patience!"

The ninth month was about to begin! The entire kingdom was abuzz that the sethani was about to give birth. Lakhs of rupees would be gifted. Mountains of jaggery would be given out. Who knew if there were enough dates and sweets in the markets! But was the seth some small man? From distant lands he would order entire caravans! Everywhere, servants and beggars began to await that auspicious day.

Soon people began falling over each other to see the seth's lucky face! Even two hours after nightfall, they would be clamouring at his haveli as if it were a carnival. The seth would oblige them by standing on a platform and giving his *darsan*.[1] People would see his face and then look at the sun. In the evening, when lamps were being lit, the same crowds thronged still. The seth was so fond of giving his darsan that he would not even eat on time After all, that incident with the farmer on Akha Teej still stung his heart.

In the ninth month, the sethani drew the curtains and lay down. The priests and pandits now barred even the seth from seeing her. The seth was reluctant, but when the sethani insisted, he had to agree. He would stand behind the curtains and ask the naayan for any news every hour.

The astrologers and pandits read their charts and declared that tomorrow, when nine months would end, if the seth as much as even climbed the stairs,

---

[1] Also written as darshan, meaning 'lining up to see a holy image or deity'

the life of the *jaccha*[1] would be endangered, and if the mother's screams or the child's cries fell on anyone's ears, the child's life would be in danger. When the naayan explained that these were the sethani's orders, the seth had to agree.

And on the night before the full moon, the bronze thaals were clanged for two hours! The servants in the haveli were all waiting for this. The sounds of thaals and yet more thaals arose. The clamouring crowds outside began to clang bronze thaals with such excitement that countless thaals were broken. As if the wind was stuck mid-air! The sky itself descended with its nine lakh stars.

And what to say about the *nichrawal!*[2] Of money, of dates, of misri[3] and dried fruits! For seven days, the same festivities! The same merriness! The same carnival! But it did not make even the slightest difference to the seth's wealth.

The astrological charts were consulted. The royal astrologer first read them—no cause for worry! All the pandits just said one thing—the child's future was as bright as the sun, but for the first twelve years of his life, the alignments of the stars were to be hard on him.

---

[1] A new mother; a woman who has recently given birth
[2] Gifts distributed on happy occasions
[3] Sugar crystals

112

If anyone saw his face even by mistake, his life would be in danger.

Who would take such a risk? Nine months had passed—how long would these twelve years take to fly past! All the seven contentments of human life were now his with the coming of this son. Surely these years would also pass in the blink of an eye.

Special things were made for the new mother. For the first seven days, ajwain[1] and sweets. Then laddoos made of powdered and dried ginger, goond[2] and flour. Laddoos made of almonds. And with the sethani, the stores were opened up to thousands of jacchas. Delicacies for new mothers began to leave the haveli around-the-clock. This is the pomp of the birth of a child in a rich household! New mothers who have been poor since birth do not even get sour rabdi to drink. Rather than that hell, childlessness is better. Why do the poor even marry and why do they give birth! Even the baby born of a sheep is better off! Now one knows what is a carnival on the birth of a new being!

Here the entire kingdom was engulfed in the commotion of celebrations, and there behind the curtains, the jaccha-rani was stuck in a strange dilemma. That day on Akha Teej, that farmer, wary

---

[1] Carom seeds

[2] Resin of a tree, used to make sweets

of the ill omen of seeing a childless person, had spat and turned around immediately, and the seth had almost lost his senses. The seth had cupped his head and slumped to the ground. Then he fainted on the ground itself. Crores worth of wealth locked up safely in his vaults, but there he lay on the road, his head swimming, his jaw clasped tight, his eyes gaping. Flies buzzed around his head looking at the state of the wealthy seth! At dawn when people started to move to and fro on the roads, they had found him and carried him home. What a state! How did this come about! The power and warmth of boundless wealth was of no use. And when the sethani heard everything in the seth's choked voice, every pore of her body had started crying. In that time of grief, how much could two poor eyes cry! What were they! The sethani began to think of ways to wipe out this grief in her husband's heart. Either she would have to conceive or she would have to deceive! And keep him deceived!

At that time, there was nothing purer than that deception! But she hadn't even dreamed that that day's lie would land her here! And hadn't it only just begun? Now how would she keep up this deception? And how would she keep living it? For how long? This trick, conceived to appease her husband, would surely be exposed one day or the other! What state would the seth be in then? In the face of such pain, poor death was hardly a pain at all! But that day, the sethani had no other way out. What could she have done? *Is this a life worth living! But then when has death come when one wishes for it?* Other than this deception, what other inspiration could she find in her life? But where this would take them, she had no clue. At least this deception brought some pleasure to their lives. Then again, how long would this pleasure last? The boundless pleasure of this jaccha of deception could not be known by real jacchas even if they laboured through a hundred births!

That day she had conceived this deception with a true heart only for the happiness of her husband. But now, for her, there was no pleasure bigger than keeping up the deception itself. If she could sustain it as long as she lived, she would have lived a hundred thousand pleasures in this life. More than being a mother, the imagination of being a mother had so much pleasure in it that there wasn't so much pleasure in anything else! Not in a kingdom, not in boundless wealth and not in a large, thriving family. This deception was the best in the world. In the pitch darkness of a moonless night, the hope that at dawn, the sun will rise and on rising, destroy the darkness in an instant—the pleasure in *this* hope—where is there such pleasure in the glowing ball of the sun itself . . . ?

Parents bear the death of a young married son by beating their heads and chests! Finally, they wipe their tears with their own hands! When the father heads back home after burning the body of his young son, there is no more meaning to the drama of wailing and howling. This is all but a commotion of selfishness. After twelve days of mourning, things slowly return to normal—eating-drinking, smiling-laughing, toiling-earning and waking-sleeping. Everything goes back to where it was. Back to the same chores and back to the same chaos. But if *this* child of deception were to die, then the parents would never stop mourning. Even if the parents died, their tears wouldn't dry! Their ashes in Gangaji would weep for years! Their embers in the graveyard would burn for ages and ages.

Now, as far as possible, this deception would have to be kept up. But where was this deception a deception any more; it was the true essence of life! If it was deception, how could the sethani's breasts fill with milk without her womb conceiving! Now, the seth was engrossed in *his* truth, and his wife was engrossed in *her* deception. The sun was engrossed in its rising and setting. The seasons were engrossed in their cycles. The clouds were engrossed in their thunder, lightning and pouring. Plants in their greenness, the moon in its moonshine and its waxing-waning. And the human race was engrossed in its toil!

Who wouldn't want to marry their daughter to the son of such a wealthy seth? Proposals started to come from every corner of the kingdom. The silly seth would say yes to every proposal! The sethani would then send a message to the Seth with the naayan: what silliness was he up to! One son and the seth wouldn't say no to anyone! "The alignments of the stars and planets are hard on our son for twelve years, and these will have to pass first," she told him finally, and after this, the Seth stopped saying yes to anyone.

The sethani would often walk around on the roof after midnight. Seeing the moon, she would feel that the moon itself was her son. Raining moonshine from up in the sky! Sometimes from the jharokha, she would see the rising or the setting sun and feel that it was her son rising and setting like this! Who could match him?

In this manner, those twelve happy years passed by with the clap of the hand. Again, proposal after proposal started pouring in. The sethani eventually thought of a plan. She sent a message with the naayan that the proposal must be from a household with one daughter only. She must agree not to be able to see her husband's face till he turned sixteen. Must accept the sun and the moon as her husband. Only with her would a match be accepted.

Clever people find clever people, and naughty people end up finding naughty people! Eventually, such a girl was found in the home of a poor baniya. If the sun was kept in the palm of one's hand and the entire world was searched and a girl as beautiful and talented was found, then her family was ready to toil for the seth for the rest of their lives! The girl was only the dowry and the girl was only the beendni. Other than this they had nothing to offer, so where would they give a dowry from!

Twelve years had passed by in a flash, so how much longer could a further four years take? With drums, music and much merriment, the seth's son's jaan left. Chariots, carriages, bullock carts and palanquins. Crimson flowers on the bullocks. Colourful threads on their horns. Scarlet nose rings. Necklaces of little bells around their necks.

A golden chariot drove up to the haveli and stood there. Even at this time, the sethani would not let even the baby of a bird see so much as the shadow of the beend,[1] leave aside the beend himself. The sethani and the naayan together made a large doll of flour dough. It was as large as a full-grown, well-built man. With hands where hands should be. They dressed it in a silken jama.[2] An orange turban. Anklets on the legs. A navlakha necklace around the neck. Earrings

---

[1] Groom
[2] Kurta

118

encrusted with pearls adorned its ears, rings set with priceless gems were on its fingers and bracelets on the wrists.

The sethani sat with that beend made out of flour in her lap. And made the naayan sit beside her. And when the jaan departed, it kicked up so much dust, it felt as if the earth had parted and spewed forth clouds of dust.

The sethani sat cross-legged in her velvet-lined carriage. No crack for even a ray of sunlight to come in. And in her lap, the boy of flour dough. Dressed as a groom. The jaan kept moving forward. But the sethani wasn't at peace for even a second! Every second felt like a lifetime.

The next day, the jaan paused beside a pond next to a huge banyan tree. Water as clean and pure as a white lotus. Dense shade. To gurgle and wash, bathe and scrub and cook and drink; what more pleasant place could there be! If they could eat rotis, rest for a bit and then set forth, they would reach their destination by evening.

Leaving aside the golden chariot of the beend, everyone else dismounted. Soon everyone was engrossed in their chores. When the seth called from some distance, the naayan got down. The sethani was still lost in the thoughts of her deception. She had no consciousness of the world outside her.

In that pond lived a naag-naagan.[1] Hearing the chaos of the wedding party, the ringing of the necklaces of bells, the sounds of the bullocks, the chatter of the people, the two came outside. Never before had they seen such a sight! Crimson flowers gleamed as the sun's rays fell on them. And the golden chariot was like a little sun itself, shining so brightly. Their eyes almost popped out! The golden chariot was parked some distance from the pond. The naagan began to say, "If there is to be a jaan, it should be like this! Such a glorious jaan! Ram knows what the beend must be like! I cannot but go and see him."

"This is the problem with you. Anything you see, your heart gets fixated on. Why pretend you don't know the terms between man and serpents even though you do? If they crush you to pulp by beating you with stones, then you will lose your life and my home will lose its luck! Why plan such mischief? See the jaan from a distance; that is enough."

Shaking her head, the naagan said, "Uh hu, I won't be at peace unless I see the beend once."

"You know and your peace knows. Now of course you won't understand however much I try. Listen, be

---

[1] A serpentine couple that find common reference in Indian mythology and folklore

120

very careful. I am waiting here. Once you return, we will go inside together."

Thereafter, the naagan did not wait for a second. She slithered into the beend's golden chariot. *This is a mother's love! Such a big lad and he still sits with him in her lap . . . But wait . . . why are the beend's eyes stony like this? And why is the mother lost like this?* The naagan stared intently. *Arre! This is a heap of flour dough! What sorcery is this! How will the toran be tied! How will the feras happen! The poor beendni's misfortune!*

The naagan's heart trembled. Her eyes became teary. In her fangs, instead of poison, nectar began to flow. What was the need for such treachery! She returned back to the naag and said in a choked voice, "The groom is as useless as the jaan is grand! He is not even living. He's made of flour dough. My brain just can't understand what this bizarreness is!"

"In this world, many a bizarre thing happens. What all will you worry about?" asked the naag. "The people in the procession know; it's their job to worry. Is there an end to God's own tricks that there would be an end to the tricks of nasty humans."

"But my heart burns for that beendni. With such hopes she must be waiting, and how they will be crushed! You are powerful; find some way or the other. If your heart is pure like mine, this thing would hardly be an issue. You have never refused me; please listen to me this time too. I won't ever insist on anything ever again. Do something to put a jeev in the groom. Else this grief won't leave me as long as I live!"

The naag hissed a couple of times and said, "Now what do I do and what do I not do! Whenever you feel like it, you begin insisting. And then you won't rest as long as I don't agree. And if I am to agree, what all do I keep agreeing to! There must be some end!"

Then after thinking for a bit, he spoke again. "There is only one solution. I can put my own jeev into this doll. Only then will it become living. But you might repent later, so think properly now. Such a handsome groom none would have seen nor heard of. The beendni will think that at least she has got a beend who matches her in beauty."

As soon as she heard this plan, the naagan was delighted. She thought of neither the past nor the future and gleefully agreed. She said, "Then who do you wait for! If I ever insist on anything ever again, you remind me."

The naag cross-checked, "See, later if you throw a tantrum, it's your problem. Don't you blame me. Think through it calmly once more."

"What is there to think of time and again? I have thought what I had to!"

After this answer, there was nothing left for the naag to further think about. He slithered towards the golden chariot. Carefully avoiding being sighted, he entered the chariot. The naagan's description of the beend was actually true.

Then a bizarre spectacle happened. As soon as the naag became invisible, the doll became living. And the first words that left his mouth were, "Ma, ma!"

The mother's trance broke. She blinked, thinking this was a dream. The inside of the chariot was aglow with the radiance of her son's face. He put his hand around her neck and said once again, "Ma, ma!"

The creator has no such measure to measure this joy of the mother! A thousand births had become fruitful. Countless lotuses bloomed in her heart. Her doll of deception had finally spoken.

The mother and her now-living son alighted from the chariot together. The seth was looking in their direction. He couldn't believe what he was seeing. He rubbed his eyes and looked again. He then rushed forward. Before hugging him, his son touched his feet, lay on the ground in front of him and touched his head at his father's feet seven times. The husband and wife just stared at each other as if they couldn't believe their eyes! Poor voice . . . Who was she to blabber at such a moment! Whenever silence does what the voice is supposed to do, the voice becomes tongue-tied. Not even a sound emanates.

Seeing the groom, the naagan was no less pleased. She kept staring at him with eyes brimming with nectar.

As for processioners—neither did their mind do their bidding nor did their eyes. A silly pair of eyes was not enough to see such beauty. Why, one needs sixteen eyes, each like the sun, to look at such beauty!

The jaan thereafter did not stop for another instant. The oxen raced ahead. At the bank of the pond, the naagan stood looking at the procession. Before today, the naag-naagan had never separated. And when they had, it was for such a high and pure purpose! The naagan was not upset at all. The jaan would return on the third day. What was going to go wrong in two days after all! But yes, their house by the pond seemed strangely empty and gloomy.

And there, the camp of the jaan was engulfed in the chaos of celebrations. Like beendni, like beend. Each more beautiful than the other. On the auspicious night of the wedding, even the chandeliers looked dim against the glow of their faces.

On the fifth day, the jaan departed for its return journey back to the groom's house. In that golden chariot, instead of the mother, now sat the beendni. This pleasure and that pleasure were so different! The pleasure of a mother's lap is one, the pleasure of a wife's company is another. No similarities at all.

Amidst this pleasure, the beend-raja thought of the naagan! She would sooner die than desist from bickering. *If we avoid the pond altogether, how many days would she wait. It would be better to explain things to her properly . . . still a chance things could be settled.* The seth-sethani also wanted to stop by the pond. They wanted the newlyweds to worship the pond and pay their respects. After all, it was there that their lives had become meaningful!

And so the wedding procession stopped by the pond with great eagerness. The naagan, waiting by the bank, went inside to her home as soon as the procession halted there. How difficult these five days of separation had been! Every second had become bigger and heavier than a mountain! This much thought for the beendni was enough! After all, how can one burn one's home to light up another's?

The beend knew the naagan well. She was good-hearted, mild-natured and understanding. But wives devoted to their husbands can be very jealous! She must have been hungry and thirsty for five days! She hated being separated from her husband. No point talking about duties and responsibilities now! Would she agree or not? Poor thing was surely innocent. Could be beguiled. Had she not been innocent, how would this good fortune have come about! Thinking such things, the groom entered the pond. As soon as she saw her husband, she began sobbing. She said even as she cried, "If you cared at all for my pain, you would not have stopped there for two extra days."

The beend-raja said, "Bawali, the jaan must be seen off by the bride's side. What could I have done? Don't forget it is you who has created this mess, and now you call me names? Did I not warn you before? I tried to tell you, but you would not listen! So I had to agree. If you cared at all for me, you would not be taunting me like this. Separation from you would be so terribly painful, I had not imagined! All day, your face would haunt my eyes!"

Listening to these words from her husband's mouth, the innocent naagan forgot all her anger. Eagerly, she asked, "Really, you missed me so much? My fortune! Now, leave this body. I'll see you as you were, then only will my heart be at rest."

The beend put on a morose face and said, "In these five long days I got sick of all the dirtiness of human life! How much I missed you! But think once, to leave the beendni in this manner, it would be the biggest sin. The parents are surely going to collapse here itself! The beendni will become a sati here. What a mess you've made! Now, if you showed so much mercy that day, show mercy for some more days. Even my heart burns and suffers without you, but what can I do! Three months hence, I will find a way out and come running back to you. But if you stop me now, it will be a loss of face for you!"

"I've erred once; now you think I will err every hour?" the naagan answered. "You think I'm so innocent?"

There was not a shred of doubt about the naagan being innocent. She would trust her husband blindly. And so, she ended up trusting him once more. She stayed back at the pond alone as the beend-raja sat in a golden chariot while admiring his beendni's face.

As soon as the jaan returned to the seth's haveli, grand celebrations began. The beendni was the very incarnation of Licchmi![1] Despite there being lots of servants, she would care for her mother and father-in-law with her own hands. Would serve them herself, press her mother-in-law's legs and press her head. Respect the servants and not discriminate. Speak sweetly. Would respect the naayan as if she were her mother-in-law. Would not even drink water without asking. The son was also very obedient. A mine of virtues. Ocean of knowledge. The embodiment of mercy and charity. And with his coming, the business began to grow! In no time at all, he understood all the nuances of business.

In between the business of the markets and the sensuality of the *rangmahal*,[2] he completely forgot about the naagan. In the blink of an eye, three months passed. At the pond, the naagan would count each day of suffering as it passed. She withered away and began

---

[1] The Hindu goddess Lakshmi
[2] Private chambers

to look like a wire. Her glow dimmed. As soon as three months were over, she left the pond to look for her husband. On the third day, at midnight, she reached the rangmahal of her husband. All four corners lit up with the mellow glow of oil lamps!

Both man and wife were locked in a deep embrace. For a moment, the naagan felt a surge of anger rise up. Mad with rage, she thought of biting the wife. But the next moment, sweet nectar flowed through her heart. *Poor thing! What is her fault in all this! Then how can I do this injustice!* If the man of her own house had forgotten her, what good would it do to find fault in others? Neither did she want to interrupt the rapturous pleasure of her husband. What to do! She coiled up and sat in a ledge on the wall and began staring at their carnival of love. For a moment, she felt as if she should not touch this immortal love. That she should return whence she came. But how could she leave! She could barely even leave the ledge.

Finally, the beend and the beendni went to sleep. The naagan slithered up to the bed and woke up her husband with a flick of her tail. As soon as he saw the naagan, he remembered everything. Looking at his face, the naagan said, "Recognize me? Never knew you to be so heartless. Did you ever think what days would befall me? And why would you, when you were having such a good time?"

After becoming a human, he had become quite cunning. Without letting his real thoughts come to his lips, the beend began superficially, "If you command, I will leave at this very moment and go with you. Let her sleep over here. But in the morning, the cries that will ring out in this haveli—make sure your ears listen to them! She should have remained unmarried than savour marital bliss for just three months. What a drama of pity you have enacted! Did you listen when I tried to stop you back then? Do you remember the promise of that day? I won't say no at all! In fact, I'll do as you say!"

He had no wish at all of leaving this haveli and this rangmahal. Where else would even the dreams of such pleasures be found! He had escaped from life as a naag with such difficulty! The naagan said, "I can read your heart. Why bother lying? Even dreaming of leaving this bed and this beendni will be difficult for you. Don't be so ready to return! If I say yes, come with me; you'll collapse. You know fully well that you aren't capable of killing me, else you would not have refrained from this sin too! But I will solve my own matter! I won't blame you. Such are the pleasures of the bed! Today I wither for it, and for it your feet keep turning back! But I'll ask one thing, tell me the truth—are you really ready to leave this rangmahal and return with me . . . ?"

This time no falsehood escaped his mouth. With his head bent down, he said, "What you say is true. My heart is here . . . I can't leave this bliss now!"

The naagan's eyes welled up. "I am not at all pained listening to this truth! The beendni found happiness thanks to me, and I won't snatch it away from her. I'll only try to add to your happiness. But coming to this rangmahal, new knowledge has dawned on me. I need only three days—you just watch quietly."

It had all started from that doll of flour dough. There was no way out other than asking the mother herself. As soon as she left her husband's rangmahal, the naagan went straight to the sethani. The naayan and the sethani were engrossed in their gossip. They were about to scream on seeing this two-man-long naagan, when the naagan said, "Don't be scared of me. I will cause you no harm. I only came to ask you one thing—did you never wonder how your doll of flour dough sprang to life . . . ?"

Both of them calmed down. The sethani said, "We were just wondering about this even now. We have thought about it so much but could find no answers."

The naagan smiled. "Today I have come to give you the answer!"

Listening to the full story, both their hearts filled with nectar. The sethani hugged the naagan and wept. But those were not tears of pain; they were tears of joy! That joy had no other way to make an appearance other than tears!

The sethani also narrated everything, from her false pregnancy to what happened by the side of that pond. The naagan kept hearing and kept weeping. The world is still here because of these nectarine tears! Else destruction would have happened long back!

The sethani then hid nothing from the seth and the beendni. As soon as they heard her, both were left stunned! No limit to their joy, no limit to their surprise!

Sitting in the sethani's lap, the naagan said to the beendni, "That day I gifted you a husband. Today I will gift you pearls!"

The sethani caressed the naagan's head and said, "Only you are the Licchmi of our haveli. If you even think of leaving this haveli, I will only have food and water in my next life; you better know this!"

All the people welcomed the naagan as the elder beendni. Great celebrations took place. Again countless rupees and gifts were distributed. From that day on, the naagan became the elder bahu of the haveli. By day, she would be coiled around the neck of her husband. By night, she would assume the form of a woman. The two beendnis had such affection for each other! Each cared more for the other's happiness than their own. Both the beendnis had two-two sons who had faces as beautiful as the moon.'

Tell me, a naagan in whose fangs flows such nectar, who could be scared of her? When kids would get the chance, they would play with her. Women would worship her. Light incense sticks and make offerings of sindoor. Then what is the big deal in feeding her saffron milk with a spoon of gold? This naagan was such a good woman that if she bit a dead man, he would come alive again! Only if the lines of such people prosper, will the race of humans be happy and peaceful.

As he chugged on his hookah, Viliyo looked at the choudhary and began saying, 'In the markets, the strange spectacle, which surprised you so, meant this. Each will find meaning in this as per his wisdom! No one said a word throughout the story. Everyone just sat quietly and listened—this is a very good thing. This is a test of the greatness of a story! And to tell you the truth, I have a bad habit—I really dislike murmur while a story is being told! In a manner, appreciation during a story adds to its beauty, but it doesn't work for me. I don't like troubling people, so I happily take what they give me. But these stories are invaluable! You see these golden flowers? If someone gifts me a pearl for every letter, I still wouldn't take it! When I tell a new story, Viliyo, the barber, doesn't stay the same person. Keeps changing! You all just stare at my face, but you do not know my heart! Now eat your rotis to your heart's fill, then burp! Drink. These subtle things you all cannot understand the essence of! Why ask the way to a village you don't have to go to?'

Eternal Hope

'In the fourth volume, there is a story, "Aasa Amardhan".
A tale of immense hardship and sorrow. It always has
a profound effect on readers and listeners . . . For the
knowledge of all the learned people gathered here,
I heard this story from the Late Bhojaram Beniwal . . .'

—Bijji

About two miles away from a certain village was a
settlement of seervis.[1] About sixty bighas[2] of barren
farmland. In Marwar, instead of water, the clouds pour
droughts every second or third year. To escape this misery,
a seervi borrowed money from a baniya at a steep interest

---

[1] A caste, mainly occupied in farming
[2] A measure of land, about 0.6 acres

rate to dig a well. Can a goat caught between the knees of a butcher escape his knife that a farmer of Marwar would escape from the books of a baniya? Digging of a well, borrowing from the baniya, barren land below his feet, rainless clouds above his head and a wife who gave birth every year in his home—if God gets trapped in these five troubles, even he would have to accept defeat a hundred times over; then what was the poor cursed-at-birth farmer of Marwar!

In the midst of this endless suffering of generations, yet another tragedy befell the seervi. His wife, the seervan, who gave birth every year, escaped from this earthly hell after two years of their marriage and left behind two wailing troubles. Her life surely improved. But the man's brothers and community members together played yet another trick on the seervi. Showing concern, they got him remarried.

The arrival of a stepmother is much worse for children than the death of their mother! What did those innocent children know what a mother's love is! They thought this new mother was their own. The arrival of a stepmother even changes the father's gaze. The two-year-old sister, crying and sobbing, bearing the beatings of her stepmother, eventually learnt how to tend to her year-old brother. In the shedding of those tears, and the bearing of the stepmother's smacks, one year passed by. The sister turned three and the brother, two. Seeing the sister and brother shed such tears every day even Saavan-Bhadua got scared of raining. The hungry and thirsty eyes of the farmers stared and stared at the skies, but the clouds were nowhere to be seen. The water in the wells also comes from the clouds after all.

The interest on the baniya's money was running, but the well ran dry. And streams gushed forth from the seervi's eyes. Had the springs in his eyes also dried up along with the water in the wells, bearing the scorching flames of hardship would have been impossible.

The husband and wife decided to go to the Malwa region. 'If we take these messengers of doom with us,' said the wife, 'then even in Malwa, we won't be able to manage. Let's just finish them off and slip out—that will be best.'

The seervi hesitated. 'How can one kill one's children with one's own hands?'

The wife eagerly said, 'You don't even need to touch them. I will finish off everything, in secret.'

The seervi almost choked. Then in a hesitating, trembling voice, he said, 'I cannot agree to such a sin! I am very soft-hearted. I am not as brave as you.'

'Why walk around pointlessly wearing these sixteen yards of cotton on your head?' she taunted. 'Wear bangles and a skirt. It was a big mistake to even ask you.' Saying this, the wife started to head back into the hut.

The seervi ran and caught her hand. 'Good woman,' he said, choking, 'if not on the kids, at least have some pity on me. Why take on this sin of child murder? If you agree, I can tell you a plan.'

'Keep your plan to yourself,' she snapped. 'Even if I die, I won't take these snakelets with me.'

'When did I ask you to take them with us!' he began. 'There's a way by which the sin of murder will not be on our hands and we will be free of these children as well. If I tell you such a plan, will you agree?'

Somewhat cooling down, the wife replied, 'If you first explain, I can try to understand—if it is worth agreeing to, I surely will. Tell me, have I ever not listened to you?'

Indulging his wife, he said, 'Who can compare with you? You are the Licchmi of my house. Eight to ten sogras[1] and a pot of raab[2] is all it will take. We will leave for Malwa today itself and lock the kids inside the hut. We will hang the rotis and the raab inside and entrust these children to their fate. But while leaving, you talk to them with the love of a mother: say that we are leaving in the morning and will return in the evening. These deceived children will wait excitedly for some days. Then dying of hunger and thirst, they will wither away on their own. By beguiling them, they will not cry and wail. Tell me, have I not hatched a great plan?'

---

[1] Rotis made of bajra flour
[2] A type of porridge

'For the first time in your life, you have spoken intelligently,' the wife replied.

The seervi indulged her further. 'This intelligence is only because of your company.'

The wife was by now rather inflated by her husband's pampering. She went into the hut and began pampering the son and daughter like they were her own children. Wiped their eyes with the corner of her odhna. Washed their faces with her own hands. Put kajal in their eyes with her own hands. Caressed them. Spoke to them in a voice as sweet as jaggery. She was thinking about how these liabilities would be off her back now. If this little gesture pleased her husband, then what was the harm! If he had broken ties with his own son, how long would it take him to leave with her? She wouldn't find such an obedient husband again. As her husband had instructed, she hung five–seven sogras and a small pot of raab.

The seervi said, 'Leave another five–seven rotis. And keep a large pot of raab instead.'

Smiling, the wife said, 'What silly things you say. This food will of course not last the full year. If these snakelets last five days or ten days, it's the same thing. They will finally die, then why waste grain? You should use your brain a little at least.'

The seervi accepted his mistake. He thought that in case this woman got angry while saying farewell, she would not refrain from beating up the children. The father hidden inside the seervi's heart wanted to see his children smiling and laughing as he left. In their absence, who would see them suffer and wail and die unseen? Their deaths would not be averted by five or seven extra sogras. But at this moment if he could leave them lovingly, at least his heart would be at ease.

The wife understood what was going on in her husband's mind. To keep the word she had given him, she caressed both the children lovingly. Kissed them on the cheeks. Then in a voice as sweet as jaggery, she began saying as she smiled, 'My good dearies, don't you be naughty. Don't you fight. Your father and I will go now and come back in the evening. We will get you two toys to play with. In this basket are sogras and in that pot, raab. When you are hungry, you eat. And on that shelf is a pot of water. When you get thirsty, you drink.'

The basket and the pots were kept so high that there was no question of the brother or the sister being able to reach them. But the two knew nothing of such things. But despite knowing nothing, Ma's behaviour towards them was very pleasing today. Instead of beatings, this sweet voice; and in place of smacks, kisses—the children's joy knew no bounds today.

The wife looked at the daughter and said, 'You are the elder one. Be very nice to your brother. Don't fight with him for anything. Now, we're going to lock the house from the outside. We will return in the evening . . . Let's see how well you behave.'

Then the seervi took both the children in his arms and caressed them. Kissed them many times. He tried to smile, but his eyes welled up with tears. His throat choked. When she saw the colour of her father's face, the daughter turned to her mother, and began to lisp, 'Look here, Ma, Kaka cries. Why wolly about us when you will find us playing in the evening? I will play with my bhai and keep him vely happy.'

The son began playing with his father's beard. 'Why spill all your love in vain?' said the wife as she lost her patience. 'Let's go; why delay so much?'

On being told off by his wife, the seervi came back to his senses. He put down the children and then, looking at his wife, he said, 'Good woman, I pray with folded hands, please keep five–seven more sogras. And a large pot filled to the rim with raab.'

'No point in all this rubbish,' she snapped. 'If we have any extra food, it will be of use to *us*. Why waste it here! All this pointless drama I don't like.'

Despite himself, the seervi spoke. 'You think this is pointless drama? Tell me, could you leave your own children like this?'

'What is this if not pointless drama? What is the big deal in leaving one's own children in this manner? Aren't *you* about to leave your own children? These are the demands of time. One must find shelter apt to the winds that blow—wise old men only have said this.'

Only the seervi knew how much respect he had for the wisdom of wise old men, but to cross his wife was beyond him.

When she heard the latch being bolted, the daughter called out from inside, 'Kaka, return early in the evening. And get toys for us.'

'Yes! Yes!' the seervi replied softly.

The wife was carrying the basket of food on her head. And then some clothes and sheets too—a load of over a *maund*.[1] As they crossed the well, she turned back and said, 'All the load is on my head, and yet it seems that your feet don't want to move.'

The seervi wanted to say something but couldn't. He hid what was in his heart and softly replied, 'The jeev finds it hard to leave behind this well that I dug with my own hands.'

'Oh, now I know!' the wife answered. 'I thought something else was the matter. But if there is no water in the well, what can we even do? If its water hadn't finished off, we wouldn't have left it . . . even if we died. We *are* dying!

---

[1] A measure of weight, equivalent to forty kilograms

If there is no water in the well, we can't dive in it and die, can we!'

The seervi said, 'Yes, what you say is correct. Water is all the maya there is in this world. Death is fine, but may God never dry up anyone's well.'

Agreeing, the seervan said, 'We suffer only because the water has dried up. Even the clouds in the sky have given up . . . then what is this poor well! In the years ahead, everything will be fine. The clouds may sulk, but they won't abandon us forever. Next year this very well will brim with water, and we will water our fields together and grow our crops. Like our land, my womb will also bear fruit. Our son will climb into your lap. Calling you Kaka.'

'Yes, this will surely happen.' Hesitatingly, the seervi began, 'In this world, everything comes to an end, but the hope in our hearts never ends . . . From this heart, hope never dries up. This sky remains suspended in nothingness for aeons only because of hope.'

Then he walked up to his wife and said, 'You must be tired. Give me the load.'

The seervan said, 'Don't you worry about the load. Just keep walking. I am not one to get tired so easily.'

And as they walked, evening fell. They stopped to rest under a large, leafy pipal tree. To the west, a scarlet evening was starting to burst forth. Lost, the seervi said, 'The kids must be waiting for us now. They will surely cry once it is night. If some merciful person hears them crying and takes them away, it would be just perfect.'

The wife sighed deeply. 'We've come such a long way and your heart is still trembling. If you are brimming with so much love, go back. Nothing has happened yet.'

The seervi shook his head. 'When did I talk of going back? But the thought of the kids is troubling the heart. I am trying to be tough, but their thoughts don't desist from flaring up.'

Cracking the bones of her fingers, the wife said, 'This is only the weakness of your heart. Even pigeons don't have such soft hearts.'

And there in the hut as the darkness of the evening began to fall, in his awkward speech, the little brother asked his sister, 'How much longer fol it to be evening? When will Kaka-Kaki come?'

Taking her brother into her arms, the sister said affectionately, 'Evening will be here only when Kaka-Kaki ale here. How can evening fall without them coming home?'

At midnight, he asked again, 'Bai, is it evening now?'

The sister patted his head. 'If it were evening, wouldn't Kaka-Kaki be here? There is still a long time for evening to come.'

And so, evening never befell that hut for a full year. Both the kids were firm in their belief that had it been evening, their parents would have returned. There were sogras and raab on the ledge and water in the pot. But both things remained untouched for twelve months. They felt neither hunger nor thirst. Every hour, the sister would tell her brother, 'If you ale hungly, don't you cry, my bhai. There ale sogras on the ledge. If you are thirsty, don't you cry. The *matki*[1] is full of watel. But the brother never felt hunger or thirst and neither did he ever cry.

He would ask his sister after every hour, 'Is it not evening yet?' And each time the sister would give the same answer: 'How could it be evening! If it were, wouldn't Kaka-Kaki have returned?'

In the rest of the world, with the passage of time the sun would rise and set. Every day, evening would come, but in the hut of these two children, for twelve months, evening never came.

After a full year, the seasons turned. In the months of Saavan-Bhadua, the clouds poured down on the earth. And how! As if there were oceans pouring forth! As soon as the water from the clouds touched it, the earth sprang forth. Both the husband and wife eagerly set back to their home. The wife had a four-month-old child in her arms now. The clouds in the sky brimmed with sweet water. The seervan brimmed with sweet milk.

As soon as they reached the side of the well near their house, the child in the wife's arms cried. Hearing its cries,

---

[1] Earthen pot

tears came to the seervi's eyes. Choking up, he said, 'Your heart is very tough. But I am soft-hearted. By now, the children must have withered away. You go inside the hut first and throw away the bodies. I can't bring myself to do it. Have this much mercy on me, and I won't forget this favour for several lifetimes.'

'Where is the mercy and favour in this?' the wife answered back. 'After all, a wife must listen to what her husband says! I would anyway have swept the hut clean of all the dust and dirt. Where is the courage in this! You play with our little one for a bit; I will take care of everything nicely.'

The wife walked quickly as her husband walked with trembling feet. As they came near the hut, they heard the sound of some murmurs coming from inside the hut. They couldn't believe their ears! They saw that the door was latched from the outside—as they had left it. They couldn't believe their eyes! Is it the leela of ghosts and spirits? Is there any end to the games of nature?

The wife pressed her ears against the door and listened carefully. A boy's voice could be heard from inside the hut. 'Bai, is it not evening yet? Why haven't Kaka-Kaki come back?'

The girl replied affectionately, 'My dear bhai, who said it is evening? If it *wele* evening, would Kaka-Kaki not have returned? Be a little patient. They will get a toy each, for both of us.'

'I will take both the toys!'

The sister patted his head. 'Of course, you can take both. Is the toy mole important than you? Now, if you feel thirsty, you tell me. And if you feel hungly, you tell me. The matki is full. The sogras and laab are on the ledge. How well behaved my brother is!'

As if someone had poured boiling hot oil into the wife's ears! In front of her, the seervi stood, stunned into silence. Was his heart full of more delight or more disappointment or more surprise? He himself had no inkling of this.

The wife opened the locks. Opened the latch. As soon as they heard the sounds of the locks, the brother and sister began jumping and clapping their hands and dancing!

'It's evening! It's evening!
Mhara Kaka-Kaki aaya!
Khunkhunia laaya!
Our Kaka-Kaki are here!
With toys for us!'

Instead of toys, the seervan landed a hard smack each on the cheeks of the brother and the sister. Biting her teeth like a demoness, she screamed, 'Villains! You still live? Haven't died yet! Even death will not hug vermin such as you!'

No sooner did these words leave the mother's mouth than both the kids collapsed in a heap right where they were. Seeing this monstrous visage of their mother, death embraced them promptly. The father tried a lot to revive them, but they did not open their eyes.

In the pot, the rotting raab was stinking. The sogras were caked over with mould. And all the water in the earthen pot on the shelf had dried up. If matkis suck up water just like this—lying on the shelf—what must happen to the throat that is dying of thirst?

The Thakar's Ghost

'I heard this story from Jagramsinghji. Of village Borunda. Caste Rajput. Aged forty-two. He heard this story from Bholaram Daroga of Borunda village.'

'. . . And I began to find a respect for the exploited classes of society. There is the scent of this in every letter of my 'Phulwari'. I was born into the Charan caste, but I have sung praises of toil and sweat and have left no stone unturned in insulting those elites who survive on the toil of others.'

—Bijji

In a certain small village lived a small thakar,[1] whose lifestyle, however, was large. This aping of the lifestyle of

---

[1] Feudal chieftain or lord

a king meant death for the villagers and the farmers! Steep taxes and unpaid labour! The people were bitter and fed up to their noses, but still they did not have the courage to leave the homes of their ancestors. And why, where would they even go? The thakar kept on aiming his arrows at the people and the people went on quietly bearing them.

But has anyone ever become the ruler of death that this thakar would? In his youth itself, he had to walk the path of death. All remedies were tried, but nothing worked. After the body was burnt, his jeev had its freedom, but it did not leave the borders of that land. The jeev of the thakar kept wandering around kair,[1] khejdi, banyan and pipal trees; and wells, lakes and ponds. Soon everyone in that village found out that the thakar had become a ghost and would wander the land, from one place to another.

In that land, there was only one big farmer who paid a thousand sacks of grain in taxes. But the officials of the estate left no stone unturned in making him suffer! The family toiled day and night but still just about managed to survive. Generations had turned to dust and mixed with that soil, but still they never had excess!

One day, this village-choudhary was headed to his fields with a spade to observe the auspicious day of Akha Teej. In a basket on his head were a pot of sweets, five sogras, gawaar[2] saag and a pitcher of cool water. He was near his

---

[1] A tree native to the desert
[2] Also spelled as *guar*, meaning 'cluster beans'

fields when suddenly a partridge called out. This was surely not a good omen! He paused where he was for a while and then started again. This time he heard no partridge.

As he walked farther, the choudhary's eyes fell on a man clad in white standing under the khejdi tree. He went near him but could not quite recognize him. Greeting the man, he said aloud, 'Who are you, ae? Didn't recognize you . . .'

The man in white smiled. 'Choudhary! Your head has swelled up quite quickly, re! Didn't imagine you'd forget the ruler of your village quite so fast. Not even three fortnights have passed since I died.'

As soon as he heard this, the choudhary understood that this was thakarsa's *bhoot*![1] Being scared would not help, he understood that. Mustering courage, he said, 'Annadata, I did have some doubt at first. But then I thought surely you must be ruling somewhere in heaven. It is lowly illiterates like us who become ghosts and spirits and wander around!'

Seeing the choudhary's softness, the ghost also cooled down. Thinking, he said, 'Choudhary, I ruled enough while living. Now I have no desire to rule. If I told you the truth, you would not believe me . . . I rejected the rule of heaven only for the benefit of you farmers. I gave you enough hardship while living. Now, I will guard your fields as a ghost. Should pay off at least some of my debts.'

The choudhary clucked, 'Annadata, why put such weight on us ants! We were born so that our rulers could

---

[1] 'Ghost' in Hindi

rest. We are your hands and feet; we toil day and night for you. Where is the hardship in this!'

The thakar's bhoot began to say in a sweet voice, 'No, re, choudhary. While living, things were different. Death has put my brain in its place. For our sake, how much I made all of you suffer! In death, not even a fistful of grain accompanies me. Had to leave the palace behind. The priests and pandits perform puja every day to ward me off. Why would the rajkanwar and the thakarani[1] have anything to do with me! All are the games of self-interest! I desire so much to go back into the fort, but they won't even let me set foot there. Now I regret that for these people I made you suffer so much. If in some way I can pay off your debts, I will be at peace.'

The choudhary's heart melted. He had never heard such sweet words from his ruler's mouth. With folded hands, he said, 'As soon as your royal mouth said the words, the debts were repaid.'

The thakar's bhoot interrupted, 'Debts are not repaid by empty words. I really do want to repay my debts. Tell me, choudhary, every year, how much harvest do you reap?'

'Annadata, is this hidden from you! If the weather is favourable, never less than a thousand maunds,' the choudhary replied.

'But you would be left with barely a hundred maunds. My jeev now trembles at how much I tortured you all!

---

[1] Wife of the feudal chieftain or lord

You listen to me—no need to even dig the fields. You return as you came. It is now my job to harvest two thousand maunds of bajri in the harvest season. Don't send even a single grain to the fort. Those people deserve this only!'

The choudhary shook his head. 'Ni, Annadata, ni, may Ram save us from such earnings! How can we animals live as you fortunates? Hearing such nectar-like words from Your Majesty's mouth, I have earned not two thousand but two lakh maunds of bajri. Annadata, we illiterates have for generations eaten what we grow with our own hands. There is no way we can digest this grain that we haven't earned! To sit around vacant and jobless, to me, is worse than death!'

The thakar was annoyed with what the choudhary said. But suppressing his anger, he said, 'What! You want to say that only us thakars and royals can digest the toil of others? We eat the earning of *haram*[1] . . . ?'

The choudhary folded his hands up to his elbows and bowed down. 'I could never say such a thing! Have I a rented mouth that it will say such nasty things about our rulers? The work of the fortunate is to rest; this is the karma of your last life! And it is our karma that in this life we toil and labour. Your Majesty has offered to help—is this a small mercy?'

The bhoot came near. Biting his lips, he said, 'All this empty mercy means nothing. Now my deeds will speak!

---

[1] Illegitimate or not acceptable

There's no need for you to as much as face your fields. Sitting-sitting, when two thousand maunds of bajri will reach you, only then will you know the full extent of my mercy. You farmers should also once taste the pain of rest! We have been bearing it for generations!'

The choudhary was now in a dilemma. Neither did he want to take the bajri that he hadn't earned nor did he want to argue too much with this ghost. And that too the ghost of the thakar! If it got angry, it could uproot the entire family. After thinking it through, he finally said, 'Annadata, let me at least observe the lucky omens of Akha Teej.'

The bhoot shook his head. 'I have appeared to you after death; what further lucky omens are left after this! Two thousand maunds of bajri is certain. Go home and snore. No need to even look at your fields.'

When the thakar's ghost would just not agree, the choudhary returned without even touching the soil of his fields with his spade. He had seen many a miracle performed by ghosts and spirits. For them, nothing was too difficult. If the ghost had promised to harvest two thousand maunds of bajri, he surely would. But the farmer was not very happy. How could he accept this bajri that he had not earned!

He reached home and hid nothing from the choudharan.[1] He told her everything in detail. The choudharan flared

---

[1] Wife of the choudhary

up as if someone had set foot on a snake's tail! 'We don't want this rotten grain that we have not earned. The curse of laziness will not leave us for seven generations! Better to die of hunger.'

Suddenly, the choudharan began laughing amidst her rant. 'I didn't know you were so foolish. When he was alive, the thakar gave us so much suffering; in death, he will do us this favour! You may believe this; I wouldn't believe it even in a dream.'

The choudhary said, 'In front of a bhoot, even the most cunning person has to act dumb. Even I couldn't digest this, but what could I do? If he got angry, some harm might come to our grown-up son, so I didn't say much!'

As soon as she heard of the danger to her son, the choudharan also felt scared. She said, 'I haven't a shred of belief, but suppose he does fulfil his promise, we won't keep even a grain in our home. Half the bajri will be sent to the fort and half will be given to the pigeons. We will think of it as a terrible drought—that the wrath of Inder Bhagwaan has befallen us.'

The husband and wife somehow took heart. But with the arrival of the monsoon, Inder Bhagwaan was so generous that the drains overflowed. As if the clouds forgot to stop pouring. Water and more water!

After many days, the soil was again fit for tilling. All the farmers of the village set out with great eagerness with their ploughs. The choudhary also could not restrain himself.

He harnessed his Nagauri bulls[1] and left. He told all the farm hands that as soon as they would get his message, they should get eight ploughs and come straight to his fields.

The thakar's ghost was still standing below that same tree. As soon as the choudhary greeted him, the ghost began, 'I prohibited you so many times! Why have you come to plough your fields? You don't believe my words . . . ?'

The choudhary stopped his bulls and said, 'No, Baapji,[2] who am I to disbelieve you! Since I can remember, I have not seen such rains. I thought why not earn the toil of our hands? Even those grains will be your gifts to us after all. And to tell you the truth, I have never sat idle. As soon as it rained, every muscle of mine wanted to get to work! Let me plough some lines in my fields, just enough for luck, Annadata.'

The bhoot spoke as he shook his head. 'Uh hu, this time I won't even let you set foot in your fields. You people used to badmouth us—that we kings and rulers put one hand on another and enjoy life. Now you will find out how hard it is to enjoy life when one is idle! You are already sick of it! Salute me—for as long as I lived, I didn't even shoo the flies that sat on my face. A person in this world often feels his own pain and thinks that another's happiness is much bigger than it is . . . This does happen. But my heart knows

---

[1] A well-known breed of cattle
[2] Father figure

154

how it has quietly lived the pain of pretending to enjoy life. Never even let out a sigh!'

The choudhary could find no way to convince the bhoot. He returned as he had come. Neither was he allowed to pluck out weeds nor was he allowed to plough the fields. All the other fields had been neatly dug and ploughed, but the choudhary's fields were undug and the earth was hard. The choudhary said nothing to anyone. He just began to wander, looking at other people's fields. Everyone asked him the reason for his not farming his land, but he avoided answering.

When the green of bajri began to sprout forth in other's fields, his brown lifeless fields began to look ugly in comparison. But what could he do? Fretting and wandering, he went back to his fields. *This bloody bhoot never leaves that tree only!* As soon as he saw the bhoot, the choudhary wailed, 'Annadata, throughout the land, the fields are lush green, but my fields are bare. How will there be harvest without anything growing?'

Laughing, the ghost said, 'Sowing, harvesting, threshing—all this you humans have to do! Us divine beings can just wish a heap of a lakh maunds of bajri into being. Can't you people be at peace without all this hassle and hoo-ha! So clearly I commanded you, but still you won't mend your ways.'

The choudhary said morosely, 'When we go through the effort of farming and don't get anything, our hearts are at peace. But without any effort, our fields lie bare—this hurts like an arrow piercing through the heart! Annadata, it is still not too late. Let me plough my fields. I feel I will go mad sitting idle!'

The bhoot guffawed and said, 'Now you know that nothing is worse in the world than sitting idle. But back then you people would look at me with anger and jealousy! Choudhary, no pleasure in this world matches that of toil!'

The choudhary and the ghost argued a lot, but the bhoot would just not agree. He didn't even let the choudhary draw a line in his fields.

With time, the bajri in people's fields grew. First buds and then flowers. The swaying bajri looked like it would lift the earth with it and float away! When the choudhary would see his bare fields, his heart would shudder. Time and again, he would request the ghost with folded hands and beg him. But the bhoot would let him do nothing at all. When the choudhary created a lot of hullabaloo, the bhoot gritted his teeth and said, 'I wanted to see you people's state. The grain of no toil has not even reached you, and you've already created such a commotion. This is not going to be easy. We have hearts of stone to have been able to eat grains of no toil for generations, without complaint.'

The choudhary replied, 'A thousand times I hold my ears, a thousand times. Really, it is easier to be burnt alive than to sit idle. We are very happy with you rulers. Bless your hearts to be able to bear such pain.'

'When you people made me sit idle for generations and eat grains of no toil, made me suffer no end, then let me inflict this suffering on you at least once. It is only the first time, and you have created such a fuss. Every day I say no, still you keep coming back.'

The choudhary was stuck in a vicious cycle. If he went to his fields, the bhoot would not let him be, and if he was at home, he just could not be. Even as he lived, his fields were left bare. The people's fields swayed with bajri. Even atop a camel, one could not see the end of the fields, and here his fields lay as bare as a bald man's head. Soon his neighbours began to tease him. Now, the choudhary could just not stay away from his fields. But every time, the bhoot lay waiting. The choudhary kept his turban at the bhoot's feet and said, 'Annadata, if I had farmed the fields, this time there would have been two and a half thousand maunds of bajri. In fifty years such a crop has not been seen. The bajri grows as if it bursts forth from the underworld! People's fields are abuzz with so much activity that the eyes can barely take it all in. I don't see how these bare fields will give us a harvest! Even now, if you wish, any miracle can happen. Bestow me the blessing of growing bajri better than everyone. I can still toil in the fields. Let me do something. Neither does sleep befall me nor hunger!'

The bhoot said, 'This time, your stores will just fill up directly. You have to see my miracles at least!'

The choudhary bowed his head low to the bhoot's feet and said, 'Annadata, if you want to show miracles, show it in the fields. Even now, digging, sowing, weeding, reaping, threshing . . . there is a lot to do. Let me live my habit of toiling somewhat at least. Earning minus the sweat will be worse for me than poison! Leave aside two, I am happy with even one thousand maunds, but without doing anything, I feel as if a mountain weighs down on my chest.'

But the bhoot remained adamant to his word and the choudhary kept insisting on work. The bhoot said, 'If you agree, instead of two thousand, I will give you four thousand maunds, but you have to agree not to take even the name of toiling. Just imagine that you have been ill throughout the monsoon.'

The choudhary scratched his head. 'Fully fit and fine, how can I imagine that I've been ill?'

Once home, the choudhary felt dejected and listless. His heart was in nothing he did. The choudharan tried to cheer him up and joked, 'The thakar's bhoot will fulfil his word by whisking the bajri from the fields of others or what? If he has to show his miracles, why delay? Not that he has to grow the grain!' When she saw that her husband wasn't cheered up, she continued, 'Why do you fret so? If you don't want it, I won't cook even a grain in the pots! I'd rather throw it to the pigeons than do something you do not wish.'

The one thing that really pierced the choudhary's heart like the head of an arrow was that Inder Bhagwaan had blessed everyone else, and yet, his own fields were as bare as a pond in midsummer. Today mountains of stalks would have been cut and piled up in his fields. And bajri, the colour of deerskin, would have been harvested.

The choudharan tried a lot to talk of other nice things, but the choudhary's heart was not at peace. The next day, he again went to his fields like a madman. And again, the thakar's ghost appeared in front of him, smiling. 'Choudhary, today you look crestfallen. What is the matter?'

The choudhary said, 'Baapji, you reside in people's hearts. Are the flames that engulf my heart hidden from you? I beg you with folded hands—don't have the bajri sent straight to my stores, but instead, pile up stalks in my fields. I can thresh and husk the grain . . . At least this much my hands can do. Without toiling, my bones creak!'

The bhoot said, 'Now think, what must have been my state as I lay sprawled on my bed? I never so much as crinkled my nose. And you're sick of just this much rest?'

'You fortunates are different,' sighed the farmer. 'I don't even want to stop toiling after dying! As long as I live, I will be grateful . . . I will worship you. Please bestow the mercy of some work on me.'

The bhoot shook his head. 'Once I've said no, the same mouth won't say yes. And if the matter hadn't stretched like it has, how would you have known the pain of us fortunates?

You think of neither a second nor a third thing; the bajri given to you will be excellent.'

What could the choudhary have done? Quietly, he set off for his home. The choudharan tried a lot to cheer her husband up, but all was in vain. For three days, he wistfully and mutely sat in the shed. Then on the fourth day, once more he went to that tree. The sun was high in the sky. This thakar just doesn't leave!

The choudhary greeted him and began saying, 'Annadata, if you don't listen to this request, I will kill myself. People tire of pulling their bajri-filled carts home. What a season it has been! As if the rain has moulded bajri in the moulds of pearls. Please just stack up all the bajri here. Let me at least take it back in carts.'

This time, the thakar heard what the choudhary said and laughed for a while. Even as he laughed, he said, 'Choudhary, I've seen many a silly person in this world but never seen a madman like you. You believed me when I said that I will hand over the bajri as promised! Fool, as long as I lived I inflicted pain on you people. Would it not spoil my afterlife if I gave you happiness after death! If I hadn't made that promise, you would have surely farmed your lands. And your harvest would have been the best in the land. Would I have been able to stand this? Now, you husband and wife will only see the bajri in your dreams! In your dreams . . . !'

But listening to the bhoot's words, the choudhary cheered up. 'You've saved us, Annadata! Now this mountain of suffering has lifted from my head! I don't worry at all that I will get no grain. It would have been a cause for worry if I had indeed got the grain! The earth and our sweat get along very well. If we live, we will harvest enough bajri in our lives. The coming grain of no toil has been averted! Why! I will distribute jaggery today!'

Saying this, the choudhary bade farewell and returned to his home, light as a flower. When the choudharan saw her husband's glowing face, she was delighted. 'Seems the thakar's bhoot has gone away, but not a single grain has come home!'

The choudhary spoke as if he were shedding pearls instead of words. 'This delight is precisely because neither has a single grain come home nor will it! Even death has not made the thakar forget his ways!' After this, the choudhary patiently explained everything.

The choudharan was also delighted! 'As long as he lived, he looted us with the excuse of taxes; after dying he didn't let us farm a single grain. What else could he even do! God saved us that not a single grain of no toil went down the throats of our children!'

After many sleepless nights, deep sleep befell the choudhary that night. Sweet and pleasing dreams visited him. In those dreams, he toiled and toiled. Toiled and sweated. And from the sweat grew many an invaluable pearl!

The Gulgula Tree

'I was told this story by Gavri Bai. Daughter of Harjiram Bhambi. Village Borunda. Seventeen years old. She heard this story from her ma and her nani as a child.'

—Bijji

There was a widowed mother who had one son. Handsome. Fair. Lean. Well-built body. Large eyes. Sharp nose. Teeth as white as pearls. Pink gums. Sweet voice. Long neck. And on his head, a crown of jet-black silken hair. Every day as soon as he woke up, his mother would spit at him seven times to ward off the evil eye. She would put kajal in his eyes and would put black spots on his face to ward off the evil eye—she would do quite a few enchantments and rituals.

One day, the mother decided to observe a fast. The son thought that this fast must be some great thing, so even he decided to fast. He told his mother, 'Ma, even I will fast.'

Ma said, 'Ni, beta, you must not fast. Your soft body will wilt.'

The son interrupted, 'Then why do you fast? You are weaker than me.'

'What of me, beta? I'm a closed book. I live by seeing your face . . . This life has been bad. Now I want to improve my next.'

Hearing his ma, the son said that he too wanted to improve his next life. The mother spat at him to ward off the evil eye and said, 'Beta, this life of yours will itself be as long as a thousand births. Why do you worry about the next?'

But when he kept on insisting, she thought of something. The son was exceptionally fond of eating *gulgulas*.[1] 'My dear son is very well behaved,' she began. 'I will make you the sweetest gulgulas. Mark my words, you'll eat your fingers with the gulgulas . . . You'll see!'

As soon as he heard about gulgulas, the son forgot all about the fast. He began longing for the gulgulas. The mother melted some jaggery from Malwa in a pan and prepared a thin batter. In a pan, she put a layer of linseed oil

---

[1] Fried, sweetened pakoras traditionally made with jaggery

as thin as a parrot's wing and fried seven gulgulas for her son. The son felt as if he had laid his hands on the treasure of Kuber[1]!

Jumping around in the aangan of the house, he finished off six gulgulas. He put one gulgula in his pocket and left his home. He went straight to the bank of a pond. Dug out some dirt with his hand. Poured water. Buried the gulgula and began to say:

'Gulgula, gulgula, *re*,
Make sure you grow tomorrow itself,
Else I'll dig you and give you to the fair cows.'

The gulgula did not disobey the boy. The very next day it began growing. The boy again got more water. Again he started his chant:

'Gulgula, gulgula, *re*,
Grow as tall as the knees tomorrow itself,
Else I'll pluck you and throw you to the fair cows.'

And the second day, the gulgula grew as tall as his knees. Green. Rotund. Plump like a huge umbrella. The boy was delighted! He watered it again and said:

---

[1] Lord of wealth in Hindu mythology

'Gulgula, gulgula, *re*,
Grow as tall as the neck tomorrow itself,
Else I'll pluck you by your roots and throw you to the fair cows.'

And the gulgula grew as tall as his neck. Green. Soft. Leafy. Three–four times he climbed it. With great excitement, he watered it and said:

'Gulgula, gulgula, *re*,
Grow as tall as a bamboo tomorrow itself,
Else I'll pluck you and throw you to the fair cows.'

At the crack of dawn, the boy hurried to the pond. That unique gulgula tree had grown as tall as a bamboo and was swaying in the breeze. Pleasing and beautiful like a painting. He again watered it with fistfuls of water. Then catching a sprig of leaves, he said:

'Gulgula, gulgula, *re*,
Sprout branches from branches tomorrow itself,
Else I'll cut you with an axe and throw you to the fair cows.'

The next day, the gulgula tree had become so huge and dense that the boy just stared at it in awe while walking around it. His heart felt lush green. Then with his fingers, he dug deeper around its base. He watered it all day with fistfuls of water. In the evening, as he left for home, he said:

'Gulgula, gulgula, *re*,
Every leaf must touch another tomorrow itself,
Else I'll dig you out by your roots, chop you up and
    throw you to the fair cows.'

And the next day itself, every leaf touched another. The pond
was now more beautiful than ever. The boy was mesmerized
as soon as he saw it. Travellers spat at it to ward off the evil
eye. The boy now began circling it like a buzzing insect.
Inspected every leaf. Then watered it all day with handfuls of
water. In the evening, as he left for home, he said:

'Gulgula, gulgula, *re*,
Sprout buds tomorrow itself,
Else I'll pluck you and throw you to the fair cows.'

And the next day, the scent of the buds burst forth! Everyone
who saw it was astounded. Never before had anyone seen
such an extraordinary tree. The boy was as happy as if he
had become the ruler of the world. That tree abloom with
buds swayed as if it were a dream. He watered the tree the
whole day. In the evening, as he left for home, he said:

'Gulgula, gulgula, *re*,
Every flower must touch another tomorrow itself,
Else I'll dig you out by your roots and throw you to the
    fair cows.'

And each flower touched another. The tree almost bent with their weight. No one had ever heard of such an extraordinary tree. The boy's delight knew no bounds. And with this extraordinary tree by its side, the pond became even more picturesque. The boy's neck began to hurt from looking at the flowers for so long. Then he again watered it. While leaving in the evening, he said:

'Gulgula, gulgula, *re*,
Bear the fruit of real gulgulas tomorrow itself,
Else I'll cut you with a sharp axe, chop you up and throw
     you to the fair cows.'

That night the boy could hardly close his eyes. Longing for gulgulas, he tried a lot to get some sleep but couldn't even for a wink. It was the night of the full moon. With an hour of the night left, the boy set out to the bank of the pond. When his mother kept asking where he was going, he asked her to be patient, at least till mealtime; then she would find out herself.

As soon as the boy reached the bank of the pond, the sweet smell of gulgulas wafted up to him. As if they had been fried in ghee made with cow milk. The sweet smell of gulgulas made the boy's mouth drool. The tree was indeed full of gulgulas. For quite some time, he was just stunned into silence, taking in the sweet smell of gulgulas. In that moonlit night, the gulgulas looked even more beautiful than the flowers.

As soon as the sun's rays touched them, the gulgulas began to glimmer like gold. The boy's heart could not resist the temptation for another second. He leapt on to the tree. He began plucking the gulgulas with both his hands and devouring them. They were like crystals of misri with butter! He began gulping them *gapak-gapak* without even chewing them! Ma had surely never made such gulgulas! As soon as he plucked a gulgula, another grew in its place. He alone ate as much as four grown-up men. Who in this world could possibly be more content in the world today than him?

Stomach full, he was burping, when a mother and daughter came and stood below the tree. The mother was old and withered. The daughter was about as old as the boy. Thin and fair.

The mother was bent. A stick in her hand. Then she straightened her back somewhat, and sheltering her eyes with her hands, she looked up and said, 'Beta, what kind of tree is this? I'm nearly a hundred and a quarter, I've wandered far and wide, but never have my eyes seen nor my ears heard of such a tree.'

Sitting on the gulgula tree and swaying his legs, the boy said, 'Dokri-ma, what have you even seen then! This is a gulgula tree! Planted by my hands, watered by my hands!'

The dokri said, 'Beta, did you only find me to joke with? Has there ever been a gulgula tree?'

'Can't you see the tree is laden with countless gulgulas and more gulgulas?' the boy answered.

The dokri replied, 'I can't see clearly, that is why I asked you—'

The boy interrupted, 'If you can't see clearly, ask your daughter—her eyes are as big as bowls.'

The mother turned to her daughter, who said that it seemed like they were gulgulas indeed!

The mother wiped the drool from her mouth and said, 'Beta, may Ramji make you live a thousand years. Give us mother-daughter some gulgulas to eat too. Why eat all alone?'

Today the boy was very merry. 'Where is the scarcity in gulgulas that grow on the tree?' he said with a smile. 'I'll pluck as many as you want. The gulgulas of mine grow back as you pluck them!'

The dokri was carrying a basket on her head, which was full of thorns. Long and sharp. The boy said, 'Lay out the basket, I will fill it up with gulgulas.'

The dokri clicked her tongue. 'Ni, beta, the basket is full of thorns. The gulgulas will break if they fall on them.'

'Then get a sack or something.'

'Where do we get a sack from?'

'Then spread out your cloth.'

'The cloth will become oily.'

The boy said, as he plucked gulgulas, 'Okay, fine. Spread your palms. I'll throw the gulgulas straight into them.'

Again, the dokri clicked her tongue and said, 'Ni, beta. The gulgulas are very hot. My palms will get burnt.'

The boy got irritated now. 'Then what can I do about this? You keep saying no. Why not suggest something else?'

The dokri said, 'Beta, the teeth may be thankless, but the intestines are never thankless. Even after I die, they will continue to bless you. Tie up the gulgulas in your turban. May Ram bless you.'

The boy agreed straightaway. Sitting on the gulgula tree, he cared nothing for these little things! With one end of the cloth, he tied three–four fistfuls of gulgulas. And tied the other end of the cloth to his hand.

The dokri caught hold of the end of the cloth and suddenly tugged at it hard. The boy came crashing down. Even before he came to his senses, the mother and daughter tied him up and put him in their basket. The dokri then picked up the basket herself and placed it on her head. As soon as the boy regained his senses, he began screaming. The sharp thorns pricked him. He begged the old woman to let him go, but she would not listen. Grinding her teeth, she said, 'Will you stop jumping around or not? If you wriggle too much, I will eat you raw! Do you know who I am? A daakan!'

The boy stopped crying and said, 'Did you not say that the teeth may be thankless, but the intestines are never thankless? Is this the reward for giving you gulgulas?'

Grinding her teeth, the dokri said, 'This one is surely a rascal. I've not yet even touched your gulgulas, so no question of my intestines being thankless! As if this tree belongs to your father! I will eat as many gulgulas as I want. Who are you to tell me not to? Keep your orders to yourself—won't work with me!'

The boy understood that arguing would be in vain. He would have to wait for the opportune moment. For now, it was better to survive with sweet talk.

'If by eating me, your intestines are happy, then that's a good thing!' he began. 'Rather than dying and be burnt, it's better to be food for men! My gurus teach me this every day.'

Hearing the boy's words, the dokri somewhat calmed down. Pleased, she said, 'Excellent teaching! Who is this marvellous teacher, *re*?'

The old witch was extremely pleased by the boy's fearlessness. The taste of the meat of the fearless was another thing altogether! The flesh of the fearful becomes dry. Today, after many years, the mother and daughter would have the bliss of eating a human!

Lying on thorns, the boy heard the mother and daughter talk. He soon sensed that they were passing a pond. He said, 'Daakan-ma, I'm really thirsty. My whole body bleeds.'

The daakan looked at her daughter and said, 'Good you said it now. If you had said it any later, we would have had to come back all the way.' She climbed up the bank of the pond with the boy in the basket on her head. Then laying down the basket near the bank, she said, 'Go, drink your fill; such pure and cool water you must have never drunk before!'

The boy said, 'I can't stand up because of these thorns. Please get some water for me.'

The dokri smacked the ground with her stick and roared, 'Scoundrel! Ordering me around! Get up and drink with your hands, or let it be.'

The daakan and her daughter grabbed his hands and made him stand on his legs. Thorns had pierced his body all over, but the boy did not even crinkle his nose. Quietly, he entered the pond to drink water and kept on going farther. As soon as the water reached his chest, he dived and vanished. When the daughter alerted her mother, the old woman called out, 'Look here, gulgula boy, listen to me, or else there will be no one worse than me!'

She kept on screaming, but he swam like a fish and emerged on the other bank. The pond was quite large, so there was no way they could catch him easily. As soon as he came out of the water, he started running. When he was on solid ground, the boy began to run like a horse. The daakan kept on calling him, but he ran and went back straight to the gulgula tree. He rested for a bit under its shade and again climbed back up the gulgula tree. Soon he began plucking the gulgulas and eating them.

The daakan could smell and tell that he was again sitting on the gulgula tree, eating sweet gulgulas and enjoying himself! She thought of a plan. Sending her daughter home, she changed her disguise and again passed the same tree. Her age and stoop did not change, but her face and voice changed completely. In the same way, she raised her neck, sheltered her eyes and said, 'Beta, what is this new tree? I've grown so old but still have never seen such a tree.'

The boy shot back, 'Have your eyes burst? Can't you see—it's a gulgula tree.'

The woman answered back, 'Even I could see that, beta! Why, even Ramji must not have seen a gulgula tree! If you make me taste a few, I'll know that it's the truth you speak.'

The boy got angry and said, 'Daakan-witch, get lost! This time I won't fall into your trap. Wouldn't you eat my flesh if I did?'

The dokri pretended to be surprised and closed her ears with her fingers and said, 'Beta, why do you talk as if Ram has forsaken you? I have come to the bank of this pond for the first time today. I came to find my goat. If you say, I will leave without finding it. But why talk rubbish?'

The boy stared hard at the old woman. True . . . there really was a goatskin flask full of water on her shoulders. The face was also different. *Surely, there are many bent old women*, he thought. Softening, he said, 'That daakan looked so much like you.'

The dokri laughed and said, 'Beta, you are so silly. Every goat in my herd looks the same, but their bodies and souls are all different! Why call me names? If you want, I will go my way even if I can't find my goat.'

Saying this, the dokri began to limp ahead. Seeing this, the boy was convinced that she was not that witch. He shouted, 'Dokri-ma, don't go. Where is the shortage of gulgulas? Chomp on as many as you like.'

The dokri had heard the boy fully well, but she still continued to walk. When the boy shouted again, only then did she return. 'I made a mistake in recognizing you,' he said. 'That daakan did me in rather badly, so I got angry. Open your goatskin flask. I'll fill it up with gulgulas.'

'Its mouth is too small. The gulgulas will just fall outside.'

The boy said with pride, 'My aim never misses its mark. Not even one will fall out, you'll see. However small its mouth is, it's definitely bigger than the gulgula.'

'If you throw them into the flask, the water will become greasy . . .'

'Okay, then spread your cloth.'

'The cloth is in tatters. As soon as the gulgulas fall, it will tear.'

'Okay, then spread your hands.'

'The gulgulas are hot. My hands will get burnt.'

'Then climb up the tree like me and eat.'

The dokri laughed. 'When I was your age, I had the courage to climb up to the moon, but now I can't even jump over a fence, leave alone climb a tree. You found only me to play jokes on!'

The boy shrugged. 'Then what can I do? You only say no and no. What is to be done?'

The dokri said, 'Tie them in the end of your turban cloth if your heart truly wants to feed me gulgulas . . . !'

The boy then waited no more. He tied five–seven fistfuls of gulgulas and lowered the cloth.

As she untied the knot in the cloth, she suddenly tugged so hard that the boy fell crashing to the ground. Before he regained his senses, the dokri put him in the goatskin flask and tied up its mouth. Then slinging it on her shoulders, she hurried home.

As soon as she reached her house, she bolted the door. Catching the boy by his hair, she pulled him out of the flask. 'You escaped with the excuse of your thirst!' she thundered. 'Now tell me, where will you go? Wait a little. I'll make you drink so that you will never feel thirst again!'

After having her fill of screaming at the boy, the dokri instructed her daughter to finely pound the gulgula boy with the mortar and the pestle, spice him up and cook him in the pot. She would go to the market and get something to drink. Today, after many days, there would be a smashing party!

The shop was five miles away. The dokri took her stick and hurried away. As soon as the woman left, the gulgula boy began to guffaw so loudly that he went on guffawing for a while. The daughter of the witch was now puzzled: why was this fool laughing like this at the time of his death? The beti looked at his face. Teeth as white as pearls.

Jet-black hair so smooth that even the eye would slip off it. The daakan's daughter had dirty yellow teeth. Her hair was dry and bedraggled. As much as she had tried, neither would her teeth whiten up nor would her hair become silky and black. She became jealous of the boy. She came closer to him and said, 'How are your teeth so white? And your hair so black?'

The boy said, even as he laughed, 'You wait and watch what happens. The teeth will get whiter still. The hair will get blacker still. My mother casts this spell every day. My mother and your mother have the same nature. If she had not put my head in the mortar and beat it with the pestle every day, neither would my teeth be as white nor my head as black! Earlier my teeth were yellower than yours. And my hair was like the coir of a coconut!'

The girl squealed in astonishment, 'What are you saying! Your teeth were yellower than—!'

The boy interrupted, 'Yes, yes, they were very yellow, else am I lying?'

The girl said eagerly, 'Then why delay? Do this little enchantment for me.'

The boy said, 'Till I dress as a woman and you dress as a man, this enchantment won't work.'

'Where is the big deal in that? You wear my clothes; I'll wear yours!'

The boy hadn't thought this would happen so easily. The girl eagerly changed her clothes in anticipation of the beautiful teeth and silken hair. She made him wear all her jewels and trinkets. Then the boy said, 'You'll have to plait my hair too.'

The daakan's daughter now got annoyed. 'You fuss too much! Sit down! I'll plait your hair right away,' she huffed.

She began plaiting his hair. Tresses as smooth as silk! It became hard for her to be patient for another second. She quickly parted his hair and plaited it. Looking at his face, she said, 'Leave aside my ma, even I can't say that you aren't her daughter. Look at you! If the teeth and hair become similar, no one can know who is who!'

Then she ran and got the pestle. She gave it to the boy and put her head in the mortar. Why would the boy wait any longer! As soon as he got the chance, he brought down the pestle so hard on her head that in only one scream, the girl was limp and lifeless. As the daakan was still out shopping, he quickly smashed and chopped her up and put her into the pot. He then added lots of spices and ghee.

The daakan returned from the shop in high spirits, swaying and singing. Then she suddenly remembered and asked her daughter, 'Is that rascal cooked?'

The moment the daughter said yes, the old witch sat down with a large bowl. She began saying, 'Two bowlfuls I will eat. After many days, the creases in my stomach will get ironed out!'

The daughter tilted the pot and filled the bowl. Her Ma began eating it even as it was boiling hot, and even as one looked, she finished it all off. As she began eating the second bowlful, her pet cat came and said:

'Ma eats her daughter, *haaye re haaye*,[1]
Give me a little piece, *haaye re haaye*.'

But the Ma was too happy to understand what the cat said.

As she ate, she found a little, little finger in the bowl. A four-inch-long nail! The mother was confused. This nail was certainly her daughter's. But the daughter was standing there serving her! Maybe the boy too had such nails, she thought!

She ate the meat and rolled over where she was. At midnight, she woke her daughter and said that the daughter's in-laws would come at dawn. If by chance she should wake up late, the daughter should leave no stone unturned in their reception. Even if she was a daakan, even if she was asleep, she could not forget what was important for the respect of her daughter.

And so, the daughter's in-laws came to fetch her, and at night, she was bid farewell. Parting with her daughter, the mother's heart was in her mouth. She hid and cried her heart out.

On the way, when a *dich* sound was heard from the beendni's carriage, the entire procession halted. The beendni

---

[1] Meaning 'what a shame!'

quietly got off. No one asked anything. There was nothing to ask about anyway! But when she didn't return for two hours, her in-laws panicked. They began searching for her everywhere. At last, they found all her clothes below a tree, but the beendni was nowhere to be seen. What could they do? The next day at daybreak, five–six elder men came to the daakan's home. 'Has the beendni come here?' they asked.

The dokri said, 'Why do you ask me? I had sent her off with you . . . You haven't killed her off, have you . . . ?'

When the dokri's ears heard these words from her mouth, a shiver ran through her body. As soon as the effect of the drink from last night wore off, she understood what had transpired last night. In a flash she understood what the cat had said. The nail of that little finger seemed to stab her insides! That finger was her daughter's! That devil had fed the mother her daughter and fled.

The daakan began to convulse. The fire in her heart would not be put out till she ate that gulgula boy! The rascal had tricked her the second time! Killed her daughter!

The daakan was very sure that the boy would not leave his gulgula tree and go anywhere! She again changed her appearance, took a stick in her hand and went there straightaway. As she passed from under it, she stared at the extraordinary tree and asked, 'Beta, what tree is this? Leave alone having seen with the eyes, even my ears have never heard of such a tree!'

The boy hid his anger and said sweetly, 'Ma, this is a gulgula tree.'

The dokri continued to stare and said, 'So, this tree bears gulgulas?'

'Yes, Ma. And not just any gulgulas, but gulgulas that taste as if they have been fried in ghee made with cow milk.'

She said, 'Beta, may Ram make you live a thousand years. I've only ever heard of gulgulas, never tasted them. If you give me twenty gulgulas every day, I'll worship you every single day.'

The boy said, 'Why twenty, have a thousand gulgulas every day. Why would I say no?'

The dokri replied, 'Ni, beta, I don't want thousand. Twenty is enough. Too much greed is not good.'

The boy saw that the woman carried a trunk on her shoulders. 'Come, open your box. I'll fill it up with gulgulas.'

She hesitated and said, 'Ni, beta, my clean box will become greasy.'

'Then spread your odhna.'

'My odhna is dirty . . . The gulgulas will become dirty.'

'Then spread your hands.'

Trying to act fearful, the dokri said, 'The gulgulas are hot. My palms will get blisters . . . '

The boy knew the ways of this old woman, but he pretended not to understand, and like before, he continued, 'Not this, not that, then how do I feed you the gulgulas?'

The daakan now thought that this foolish boy was walking into her trap. If this time he escaped, shame on her tribe! Promptly, she said, 'Beta, if you want to feed me gulgulas, tie them in the end of your turban cloth and throw them this way. I will taste them myself. If they are nice, I'll help you make lots of sales.'

The boy said, 'Ma, your blessings are more important than the turban cloth. Stand here. Let me pluck ripe-ripe gulgulas for you.'

As the boy said this, the dokri promptly came and stood there with her walking stick. The boy was ready to feed her gulgulas. He shouted, 'Take, dokri!'

The dokri turned out to be louder than the boy. Said doubly loudly, 'Give!'

And as soon as she said 'give', he threw a huge stone boulder from the top. The daakan collapsed into a pile. Not a sound. The boy came near and smashed her to a pulp. He then shoved her into a pit. Washed his hands and again climbed up the tree.

In some time, the boy's mother came by. When she saw her son on the tree, she was delighted. 'Ae, langoor, you sit here having a nice time and I've been searching for you for so long that my legs are swollen! At least come and eat on time.'

The son brought a fistful of gulgulas and said, 'Who would leave these gulgulas made with cow's ghee and have morsels? Now you don't need to cook at all!

See what an extraordinary gulgula tree your son has planted!'

'Planted, re, planted! Fool! Is there ever a tree of gulgulas?'

As he put one warm gulgula in his mother's mouth, he said, 'They don't compare to gulgulas made by Ma's hands, but surely these gulgulas from the tree nurtured by the son's own hands must not be too bad!'

Even as she ate gulgulas, Ma gushed, 'Such sweet gulgulas I've never had before.'

From then on, ma-beta would have their fill of gulgulas every day. And feed everyone in the village. The more they fed, the more they grew. Such was that extraordinary gulgula tree!

To Each His Own

'And to this day, with my creations, I continue to offer
dakshina to my gurus[1] . . . Even at the age of seventy-six,
I am still learning how to read and write.'

—Bijji

The same thing can bring happiness to one and grief to
another. To bring this out, we have this story.

In a village, there lived a kumbhar.[2] There were two
very good things about him. One, he was a well-known
devotee of God. And two, his talent with clay was unrivalled
in the land. Because of this devotion, people called him

---

[1] Bijji regarded Sarat Chandra Chattopadhyay, Rabindranath Tagore
and Anton Chekhov as his gurus.

[2] Potter; also a caste

Bhagatram. And because of his craftsmanship, people thought him to be an avatar of Prajapat.[1] Pots made by his hands would speak out aloud of his finesse. As if made from a mould. People would try a lot to measure and weigh the pots, but one could take a thousand pots made by him and there wouldn't be the slightest difference of even a gram in weight or a palmful in the amount of water they could hold.

He would explain to people that all knowledge resided in this soil itself. By keeping one's eyes open, one can learn those things from this soil that cannot be learnt by reading many scriptures. Kneading clay with one's feet, one always remembers that one day this soil will take us back. This thought keeps one from leaving the path of truth.

People would go to the extent of gossiping that Bhagatram had God in his hold. If he would make up his mind to do something, God would have to make it happen. But neither did Bhagatram make up his mind to do any such thing nor did God make any such thing happen for him. But the people of nearby villages would gossip no end about him.

That kumbhar was immensely proud of his craftsmanship. He would often tell his wife that if just once he could see Brahmaji moulding the creatures, birds and humans of this world, he could recreate them in the exact same way. But his wife would tell him off, saying, 'Don't you

---

[1] The Hindu creator deity Prajapati

utter such silly nonsense. You may make somewhat nice pots, but that doesn't mean you begin thinking yourself equal to Brahmaji.'

The kumbhar would laugh. 'Then what? Does Brahmaji have some jewel in his crown? You know my dreams are never ever untrue. I swear on my craft that after last night's dream, I don't see any big difference between Brahmaji and me. Brahmaji was sitting and creating this world with the same tools. You will hardly believe me that just like this, there was a wheel placed there near him. And in the same way, there was kept a tray full of clay. And nearby, the rope and the tools. He would turn the wheel this way. Put a lump of wet clay. Pull it out and then give it shape. Sitting with his legs spread out like me! Seeing Brahmaji's tools, for a second, I fell in doubt if he had stolen my tools! When he gave it the shape of a pot and kept the pot out to dry, I felt as if Brahmaji was just copying me.'

As the kumbhar painted the dry pots and pans with red and white paint, he said to his wife, 'It's pointless to tell you. You won't believe me. Just like here, there was kept a whole heap of clay. And a pit of water to knead it. Just as you are pummelling and kneading the clay, the apcharas were pummelling and kneading the clay. When I saw the same method of firing the pots, I could not stop myself from laughing. Brahmaji is just big in name only; there is nothing big in his craft at all. Same, ditto work. The same chores as us! I swear on my wheel!' He turned to her.

'Silly, what regard have you for my work! Has any dream of mine ever been untrue that this dream would be? Your man is no less than Brahmaji in any way.'

The wife held her head. 'What I feared has come to pass. Every year during summer, you need to drink ghee made from cow's milk. I've been saying this again and again, but it makes no difference to you. If your head loses it, how will this family be raised? Listen to me—start having ghee from tomorrow itself. I had come to you for some other work. But you are lost in your own dreams. Likening yourself to Brahmaji! And I see different dreams altogether. At night, I saw both our married daughters sitting with their hair untied.[1] Their heads uncovered, they were laughing loudly. With bare feet, they were doubling up with laughter. Their nails had grown as thin and sharp as thorns. Laughing in dreams is a bad sign. As soon as I opened my eyes, my heart began to burn so much that it still burns *dhapal-dhapal*! It's been two years that we have had no news from our daughters' *saasras*.[2] You are only lost in your sons. These sons won't carry you to heaven. Go and check in on our daughters once. If they send them with you, get them. I am having many bad thoughts about this dream. Good dreams of mine never come true, but these bad ones surely do.

---

[1] Women with open or untied hair were thought to be an ill omen in Rajasthan.

[2] Marital home

What does one even say about your dreams? You compare yourself to Brahmaji! As long as you live, you will not be free of this potter's wheel. And after I die, our birds won't be able to see even the trees of this village in their dreams. Set out today evening itself. Our youngest daughter can also reveal the meaning of your dream. I have never seen anyone as adept at interpreting dreams as her. Like the pots are fired in the furnace, I am burning in the fire of my dream! For heaven's sake, you are a well-known devotee of God, but you feel no attachment towards the daughters you gave birth to.'

Finally after two–three days of nagging, the kumbhari sent off her husband to meet their daughters. They had two daughters, and both were married into a village fifteen miles away. The man trudged along the way. Walking and trudging, comparing himself to Brahmaji, he finally reached the marital home of his daughters. The older daughter was wed into a family of kumbhars who made pots for a living, and the younger daughter was wed into a family of kumbhars who tilled the land for a living.

The kumbhar first went to his younger daughter's saasra. After meeting his daughter's in-laws, he met his daughter. As soon as he met her, he told his daughter about his dream and asked her about its meaning. The daughter said, 'Brahmaji is now in your control. You can get him to do what you want. He is the god above all gods. You please worship him and somehow get it to rain before the coming *Soonam*.[1] In the year before last, we were struck by drought, and last year we fell one rainfall short. Not a single grain we got. There was some fodder, which the household animals ate up. This year too things are not looking good. If we can plough our fields after Soonam, we can be somewhat sure. If this year too there is a drought, raising these animals will become very hard. You've come just in time. I hear of your praises from other people and feel so proud.'

The naive kumbhar comforted his daughter. 'As you said, Brahmaji is already in my control, so it's not like I have to buy his favour. Tomorrow is an auspicious day. From tomorrow, I will begin worshipping Brahmaji. Don't you worry about anything. Let me meet your elder sister this evening.'

The younger daughter said, 'What is the hurry? Stay for three–four days, and then go and meet her. After all, you've come a long way. You must be tired.'

But the kumbhar would not agree. In the evening, he went to his older daughter's saasra. He caressed her head and asked if she was fine and well. But before the daughter could answer, he began telling her about his dream. He added the younger daughter's explanation at the end, to which the older daughter began saying, 'Brahmaji is in your

---

[1] The ninth day of the waxing moon in the month of Aasadh. Also called *suryanavami*.

control. If you can stop it from raining till half of Saavan is has passed we'd be overwhelmed. If it rains in the latter half, we will not be harmed. But if it rains before, it'll be drought for us. It will be hard for us to fire our pots. Our pots need to be fired in the furnace. If it rains before Soonam, we will be badly hit. I am not being able to supply the needs of this village. If it doesn't rain till half of Saavan, it would a great thing. Please worship Brahmaji and have this wish of mine fulfilled.'

On hearing the conflicting wishes of his daughters, the kumbhar got lost in his thoughts. For the happiness of which of his two daughters should he worship Brahmaji? In the happiness of one was the grief of the other. And in the grief of one was the happiness of the other.

Five–seven days later, he returned to his village and gave the news of both daughters to his wife. 'If it doesn't rain, it will be drought for one daughter. But if it rains, it will be drought for the other,' he said. 'Now you tell me, for whom should I worship Brahmaji? Our younger daughter told me the meaning of my dream but could not tell me the meaning of this dilemma! I'm torn between their wishes. If you know the way out, then tell me.'

The kumbhari taunted him, 'If Brahmaji is indeed in your control, make it rain on the fields of the younger one and not rain on the furnace of the older one.' She looked at her husband's face for a while and said, 'Making it rain . . . not making it rain—let it be in whose hands it is. Nothing will come out of us messing with it. You do what is in your hands. Every summer, if you drink ghee made from cow's milk, your brain will return to its place. Then you will not have to ask anyone the meaning of such dreams. If you are fit and fine, then drought will never befall us.'

The Leaf and the Pebble

'Because I was so completely unsuccessful with love, I became very talented at writing love stories. Perhaps, had I been successful, I would not have been so.'

—Bijji

Below a tree lay a pebble. All alone. Whom to talk to? Who to speak to?

Lying there alone, he got suffocated. As fate would have it, one day, a leaf came there, flying from a distance. All of a sudden, the pebble found a chance to talk to someone. He was delighted. He accorded great honour and respect to the leaf who had come to his home.

One day, the pebble told the leaf, 'My dear friend, please don't go anywhere and leave me alone. I cannot even live a second without you now.'

'Leave a friend like you and go?' replied the leaf. 'I'm not that big a fool! But if strong winds blow, how will I stay in one place? I will have to fly with the winds.'

The pebble thought hard and finally came up with a solution. 'Don't you worry about this! I won't let you fly away even if the father of all storms passes through here. As soon as the winds blow, I will sit on you. Even if gusts of winds blow, I won't let you be blown away with it. But friend,' continued the pebble, 'in front of the rain I am powerless . . . If it pours, I'll melt.'

It was the leaf now who thought of a solution. 'Don't you worry about this! As soon as it rains, I will cover you. Even the father of rains won't be able to melt you.' And so, both friends thought of schemes to save each other.

Many a storm blew, but the pebble did not let the leaf get blown away. Many a time it rained, but the leaf did not let the stone melt.

But as fate would have it, one day, the storm and the rain came together. All the schemes that the two friends had devised to save each other proved futile. The pebble said, 'I'll save you.' And the leaf said, 'I'll save you.'

Finally, the pebble spoke up again. 'Silly, how can you save me? You'll be blown away with the first gust of wind! And I'll melt anyway. Now, let's not bother with senseless quarrel. Let me sit on you.' And so, the leaf had to let the pebble sit on it despite its wish.

The pebble positioned itself properly on the leaf.

The clouds began to thunder. Lightning began to flash. Large drops of rain began to fall. Gusts of wind began to blow. The pebble began to melt. Went on melting. Till he melted completely, he continued to protect his friend. As soon as the pebble melted completely, a gust of wind came and blew the leaf away. Tears streaming from his eyes, the leaf bid farewell to his friend with a heavy heart.

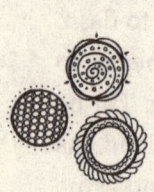
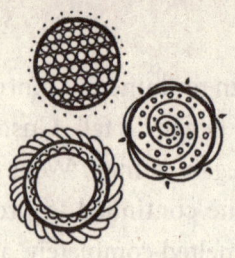

Jaraav Masi's Tales

'My village was my university, and my literary education, if any, came from rural women who always had so many interesting stories, anecdotes and wisdoms to share. When men my age went out to hunt or drink, I used to sit in my courtyard listening to what the women had to say, their gossip, their tall tales. At one point, I specifically started to invite all the women who were willing to just sit with me and talk. There were days when I was surrounded by women lost in conversations for hours at end.'

—Bijji

I was well aware of Jaraav Masi's love for motichoor laddoos and jalebis. When I came from Jodhpur, I got some packed for her. To make her extra happy, I even got some imartis[1] added in. Just the smell of the sweetmeats made Masi's nostrils quiver. As she bit on a piece of imarti, she nearly went into a trance. I think there must not have been anyone before this who had such a love for sweets! As if every pore in her body was enjoying the taste. After eating to her heart's content, she carefully hid the rest away. Licking her lips clean, she said, 'Beta! Why do you stand at my feet? Come, sit comfortably. How can I possibly inconvenience you! How precious your time is! We all go about our own work; only you write for the people of our country. Why go on slogging only for one's own stomach? Even animals don't go to sleep hungry! How many people like you are there in our country? I swear on my tongue to hide nothing from you. This tension at home will die only when I die. If you wake me even at midnight, I would never refuse you a story. Don't hide anything from me. Today, I have thought of tales to tell you.

'Today is Dhanteras.[2] Everyone will worship the goddess of wealth, Licchmiji. But you know, beta, this dearly beloved devi can neither be bound by worship nor can she be tied by faith. This is important enough to carve on to all her devotees' heads! Many think of binding her, but she isn't

---

[1] Also known as jaangiri, imarti is a sweeter and thicker form of jalebi.
[2] Dhanteras is celebrated two days before Diwali, on the thirteenth day of the waning moon in the month of Kati (Kartik).

one to yield. Many brainless people say that wealth grows because of one's karma. Even I used to believe this rubbish earlier. But after pondering for so many years, the essence I have distilled is that Licchmi is totally capricious. If she feels like it, she doesn't leave a place for generations, and when she wants to, she changes her home seventeen times a year! The rules of her game are unique from the rules of the Teen Lok.[1] One luckless person toils his whole life, even then the goddess doesn't bless him, while another who sits and warms his bed, she blesses in an instant!

'A tale must be apt to the occasion. If someone sings songs of spring during Diwali, wouldn't people chatter about his lack of a brain? At a wedding, tales of weddings are apt. Today is Licchmi Puja, and so, I will tell you of the whims of Licchmi only. Why! If Licchmi is to come, she might come even from getting kicks. Let me start with this story:

There was a jaat.[2] He married quite late. And got stuck with a mindless and foul woman. What could the poor jaat even do? That horrid woman would neither understand the norms of behaving with one's husband nor did she keep respect or regard for her husband. Every morning, she would make him sit in one place in their outer

---

[1] The three realms—heaven, hell and earth
[2] An agricultural community spread across north India

courtyard and deal him twenty-one cracking blows with her shoes. Only then would she wash her mouth! This was her daily routine. One day, the jaat said, "Licchmi! If you must beat me with shoes every day, why not take me to a locked room and hit me twenty-three times instead of twenty-one? But hitting me in broad view of the village, what pleasure do you get?"

But that stubborn woman would hear none of it. She thought that if she listened to one thing he said, he would expect her to listen to more. She said, "Before we got married, what was our agreement? Don't you feel ashamed going back on it? My shoes will deal blows like this—in full view of everyone! In some days, you will lose your shame of the neighbours and the family."

For many days, the jaat kept silent. But the village people would not stop teasing him. At the well, at gossip sessions and at doorways—everywhere the chatter was about the beatings. Boys would tease him, women would taunt him and the old and wise people would rebuke him. In frustration, he left the village that had been his family home for generations and began to live in a neighbouring city. Instead of farming, he started to work as a labourer to eke out a living.

So what if her husband went away? Nothing deterred the woman's morning routine. In the corner of the courtyard where she would make her husband sit and give him a beating, she would now deal twenty-one blows with her shoes on the stone without fail, and only then would she even drink water. Slowly, slowly with time, there started appearing a depression in the stone.

As fate would have it, a ghost lived there, in an upside-down pot—an arm's length from the stone where the jaat would sit and receive his beatings. One day, as the Jaatni[1] went about her vicious morning routine, the pot broke. And blows of torn and tattered old shoes started to rain down on the ghost's head—*fataak-fataak*! Eventually, the ghost too got sick of this and ran away. And what a twist of fate that the ghost ran to the same city where the jaat would eke out a living as a labourer!

One day, the ghost went to the jaat and greeted him. "Ram-Ram, my shoe-brother!". The jaat acknowledged the greeting, but he didn't understand the meaning of the 'shoe-brother' remark. Then the ghost explained that both had endured twenty-one beatings of the Jaatni's same old and tattered shoes, at the same spot. Didn't that make them shoe-brothers?

The jaat sighed. "Yes, brother, yes! Because of me, you also had to suffer. If one ends up with a villain of a woman, then this is the fruit! Also, that villain of

---

[1] Wife of the jaat

a woman has mighty strong arms. As the shoe would land on my head, it made me tremble to my ankles."

The ghost agreed. "Why would I have left my dwelling otherwise? That witch has made my head all soggy."

The jaat said with folded hands, "Brother, you are a ghost. If you kill her in her sleep at night, I'll never forget your favour. A son of a jaat and here I wander around as a daily wage labourer. It makes me ashamed . . . but what to do?"

The ghost sighed. "If this was possible . . . but that woman is enough to haunt even ghosts! Why, even her shadow makes me tremble. But since I have called you my brother, I will definitely think of some solution for you. From tomorrow onwards, I won't let you work as a labourer—this is my responsibility."

Frustrated, the jaat said, "If I don't labour, won't I die of hunger!"

"Listen to me at least," the ghost began. "This evening I will go and possess the son of the biggest seth in town. He will tremble and writhe and wail. No one's medicine will work. But as soon as you go and cast your spell, I will promptly leave his body. Don't you agree for anything less than ten thousand rupees from the seth. The way your devoted wife counted her shoe beatings, in the same manner, you must count the money. So much money won't finish even if you try to eat it up. After the seth's son, I will possess the rajkanwar. But you must not go near there. Greed gets one beheaded . . . Don't even lay your feet in the durbar."

The ghost did exactly as he'd promised. The next day, the entire area was abuzz with news about the seth's son. *Baids*, *hakims*[1] and magicians all tried and failed, but it made no difference to the sickness of the seth's only son. As soon as the seth heard from the jaat, the seth promised him eleven thousand rupees instead of ten. And as soon as the jaat cast his spell, the seth's son became perfectly fine. In just one day, the jaat became famous!

Here the seth's son was cured, there the rajkanwar began to writhe and wail. Chaos descended on the entire town. The king's mounted soldiers came straight to get the jaat. "Believe me, there is no special skill in my hands," pleaded the jaat. "It was just fate that the seth's son got cured instantly. I am not really an avatar of God, am I?"

Listening to the jaat's words, the diwan told the king, "Annadata, it seems the taste of money has made the jaat greedy. Ten thousand won't be enough for him."

Mad with rage, the king thundered, "When did I make money an issue? I will give him what he asks

---

[1] Physicians or healers

for. But how dare that wretch refuse point-blank! Drag him here by his hair. If he can't cure the rajkanwar, tell him clearly that I'll have him crushed alive in the oil mill. And if he does cure the rajkanwar, he can have whatever prize he asks for."

The jaat was now stuck between two deaths: on one hand was the ghost, and on the other, the king! Here the bhoot and there the raja! Compared to this, his life of a labourer was better. He would have to go with the king's guard. The jaat began to think hard. *If I refuse, there is no way the king will spare me. But if I address the ghost as my brother, he might pay some heed to what I say. But then, he will also not agree in a straightforward manner.*

As soon as he entered the palace, he raised his dhoti and took his shoes in his hands and ran towards the rajkanwar's bedchamber in a frenzy. Panting, he whispered into the rajkanwar's ear, "Bhoot-brother, the villain-woman is coming! Bhoot-brother, the witch is coming!" Saying this, the jaat turned and began to run as though his life depended on it. The ghost's soul trembled from even the shadow of that villain. *That woman has managed to ask around and found her way here.* Hearing of her, the ghost fled for dear life.

And instantly, the rajkanwar healed. The king willingly gifted the jaat five thousand gold mohurs!'

Jaraav Masi turned to me. 'This is why I tell you, son, when money is fated to come to us, it can come to us even via the beatings of a shoe! Had the jaat's wife not beaten him in broad daylight, how would he have come across such riches! Having become the owner of such wealth, the jaat forgot about the insult of the beatings. This maya is such a thing—even insult doesn't make any difference. It hides all flaws and shortcomings. With great anticipation, he headed back to his village in a grand carriage. His wife now welcomed him back with much ado. Beta, this is all the halo of maya.

"I could see it all as clearly as if looking into a mirror," the wife said to her husband. "For this maya, I did all this drama of beating you with my shoes. You would not believe me if I told you that those shoes caused me more pain than you . . . So much so that I would cry through the night." The jaat believed his wife and forgave her.

Soon, murmurs of the source of this sudden wealth spread throughout the village, and in every home, shoe beatings became a routine! At the crack of dawn, shoes began raining down on the heads of men throughout the village and for all to see. Those who had earlier teased the jaat would now sit down for their beatings with great anticipation. The jaat's household was the only exception. He would make great fun of all the people in the village. He would insult them, tell them off and taunt them to their faces, but who would listen to a lone person! Soon, everyone's heads became bald with the beatings of shoes, but where was Licchmiji and her bounty? That happy chance befell only the jaat. Even then the people of the village kept up the routine in the hope of maya. The ignorant fools knew nothing about the caprice of the goddess! That rich seth lost all that money despite earning it with his hands, then where is there maya to be found through such beatings!'

After Holi, it so happened that I was able to return to my village only a day before Diwali. The next day, the first thing I did was freshen up and head to Jaraav Masi's home. In so many days, a lot had changed. Within the courtyard, Masi had begun living in a separate shed. In a cracked voice, I could hear her sing as she spun yarn on the charkha.

I stopped for a bit and listened. Along with the song, the charkha was singing its own rhythm. I found her voice cracked with age yet very pleasing. It was all her mood—she could go on all day without stopping! Smiling, I entered her shed. Masi was lost in turning the spinning wheel and singing. Then her trance broke and she looked up. The knot on her neck had grown since I last saw her. Rest, she was fit and fine. Even though she saw me after so many days,

Masi didn't give me much attention. She turned her attention back to her wheel and huffed, 'Now your masi has no time at all to tell you tales. Go back at once.'

I knew Masi's nature too well. Quietly, I sat down on the floor.

Masi looked at me sternly. 'Why have you come here to add fuel to the fire? Isn't my family enough? Didn't you hear what I said? Just landed and planted yourself on my floor! Let me tell you, even if you plant yourself in the ground and wait here till Holi next year, I won't have time. You are earning neat money by writing stories . . . While I was living together with my family, I could tell you bits and pieces of stories. But now things have changed. It's been five months since I've been living separately in this shed . . . I am not dependent on those people. I can still raise all of them. What do they show me . . . their able-bodiedness! Why, if instead of these oafs I had given birth to stones, at least they could have been used to build something!'

Masi was now quite angry. Grinding her teeth, she continued, 'But after separating, I am more at ease now. Those serpents starved me thin. Son, one needs her husband most in old age. If he were alive today, this would not have been my state! Why, our family has enough to raise elephants, but after him, I haven't even been getting crumbs . . . How can this maya not make one deaf and blind? The love of the stomach is ultimately greater than the love of those this stomach has given birth to.

'And *you!* You are using the excuse of stories to amass maya and just bothering me on top. You can go on simpering, but now you might as well dream of stories from my mouth. What will you tell me, beta? I know this world too well. The love of maya is a thousand times more than the love for the ma who gives birth to us. If even that great charitable seth's head went awry after seeing a body of gold, then what are you!'

I kept sitting there silently, playing dumb. The old woman would flare up if I'd say anything. Even as she turned the wheel, she started telling a tale on her own:

'In some village, there was a seth, widely known for his acts of kindness, generosity and charity. Why, in front of him even God looked like a beggar. Once, this God became angry with men, and for three consecutive years, there was a great drought. It was as if the earth itself had forgotten how to flower and sprout forth. As if the clouds themselves had forgotten how to pour down. But greater than this God who killed was the seth who saved.

Everywhere he had the heart of the earth dug up and had lakes and ponds made. In every village, he had granaries stocked up with grain. Piled with fodder. Those who died their deaths is a different story, but among the rest, that mere mortal didn't let even a child perish out of hunger or thirst. It seemed that the drought just befell the earth but made no difference to animals or to humans. People forgot the name of God and began to recite the name of the seth. And the name proved so powerful that in the fourth year, there was such bountiful rain—that there had not been such a harvest in the past century. Plentiful grain and plentiful fodder. This was all due to the glow and aura of the seth's virtuousness and charity. Even birds and animals began to sing his praises. And here the seth's business began growing so that it wouldn't stop. As if wealth was raining down. And the seth's heart began to be more and more immersed in religion and charity. Whatever wealth he had was for his fellow men, animals, birds and insects. At his haveli, even a snake did not leave hungry-thirsty.

In this rotten age, when mothers starve despite having betas and bahus, who would believe that when the seth passed under a dry tree, it would turn green; if he passed over a dry river, it would begin to flow bagag-bagag with water; if he touched barren cows and buffaloes, they would begin to birth; and if he looked down a dry well, it would fill to the brim with water. Bitter fruits would become sweet as soon as he touched them, and wells with salt water would become sweet as nectar if he drank from them. The act of giving is indeed a great and powerful thing. But look at this age; see how the stars have realigned! A mother to five sons, and I have to eke out a living with my own bare hands. If we won't have droughts every year, then what will we have?

Where there is a village, there are fools as well. In that age too, most men were goddamned. It so happened that a thief came in the dead of night to steal from the seth. The seth was lying awake. When the thief realized this, he tried to escape. But the seth caught his hand and said softly, "You have jumped over the wall to come into my household, and now if you leave empty-handed, I won't say no, but it won't reflect well on you. Why did you have to sneak into my house in the dead of night? Big words suit He Who Sits Above, but whatever wealth I have belongs to you people after all."

The thief found the seth's sweet words as bitter as poison. "If all this wealth is ours, why is all this name and fame of giving yours?" he asked sharply. "People have forgotten God and chant your name instead—is that a mistake? Why do you dream with your eyes open?"

The seth replied, "This is the people's greatness. What can I possibly do about this? I tell people off. But, tell me, what is it that has upset you so?"

The thief said promptly, "Your fame spreads throughout our country, but even I am well known in our parts . . . I can't digest what people give me on their own. I am no beggar! Nor an unfortunate! I eat what

I earn with my hands. The entire world is there, begging with hands spread out. Now, if I don't take anything, would it lessen your fame?"

Hearing sounds in the courtyard, the sethani woke up and went there. The seth said, "But when did I make giving a matter of my pride! Please take whatever you will."

The thief became red with rage. "This wealth is not only yours. Once again, if you offer me as if I were a beggar, I will cut off your tongue! If you are generous and religious, you are so in your home. No need to have all this pity on me."

The seth tried a lot of cajoling, but none of it worked.

The next day, the thief again broke into the seth's house and what does he see? Mohurs and pearls were kept in the balcony outside the haveli. In the aangan were kept heaps of treasure! But the thief was also of a stubborn mind. He did not so much as touch anything. Muttering and cursing, he left empty-handed.

From that day onwards, the seth stopped hiding his maya altogether. Big and small thieves came on many an occasion. They robbed to their hearts' content. So that the thieves didn't feel any shame or embarrassment, the seth would cover his head with a sheet and pretend to snore. The world has never seen such a seth before and neither will it in the times to come.'

Masi continued spinning the wheel; there was no scope for pause. I did not even murmur in agreement with her, lest she remember that she was telling a tale. She kept on narrating as if it were a part of the chore of spinning.

'In every village and hamlet, the seth's charity was underway. The old and the disabled had their wishes fulfilled where they were. There was no living thing that could say that they didn't owe their lives to the seth. However, may Ram not make me tell lies. Animals who hunted for their food, of course, had nothing to do with the seth.

All day long, crowds thronged the seth's haveli, twelve months in a year. Animals and birds, once satiated, would head back home. But are the hunger of man's stomach and the greed of his heart ever satiated? Has the sea's thirst for water ever been quenched that man's thirst would be sated? As the seth's charity grew, the beggarliness of the race of men grew. I think leaving aside the seth's own family, there was scarcely a being that hadn't been to the seth to ask for something.

One day, during a solar eclipse, the light of the sun was anyway eclipsed, and here on the earth, hordes thronged the seth's haveli in such numbers that the dust they kicked up made it quite dark. As far as the eye could reach, there were people and more people.

It felt as if the earth would collapse under the weight of crowds. The screams and cries of the gathered hordes seemed to ring from the sky itself. That day it felt as if the world itself had turned up at the seth's doorstep.

The seth and sethani were sitting in the jharokha. "What is the meaning of such charity?" said the sethani. "Somewhere, I hope that in the false belief of charity, we aren't doing a sin. I feel charity and giving bear fruit the day it can ensure that there is no one left who needs it. But our good deeds and charity seem to have increased everyone's neediness. Even as we watch, it seems the human race has become *kangaal*.[1]"

"What can we even do about that!" replied the seth. "We can but give. If there is some deficiency in giving, please tell me."

"My understanding is that it is because of our charity that everyone has stopped working and toiling altogether," she said. "If by mere asking, wishes can be fulfilled, who would sweat it out? This has all turned out quite horribly."

Just then seven-eight of the seth's *muneems*[2] came running to him, panting. "*Dharamavtar!*[3] Murder! Murder! An old pandit has been trampled to death in

---

[1] Penniless
[2] Accountant
[3] The avatar of Dharma, or incarnation of virtue

this stampede! The terrible crime of killing a Brahmin is on us!"

The seth could only manage, "*Hain . . . E . . . E! Ar . . . E . . . E.*" He stood up. "The killing of a Brahmin? The undoing of all our good deeds! You should have been careful!"

The sethani shook her head. "The hordes extend even beyond the eye. God himself cannot care for such a crowd, then how would these people? This was the pandit's fate. Does the sin of the deaths of all priests lie on us? They die their own deaths!"

But the seth wasn't placated. He felt as if he had murdered the pandit. Now what to do! Years of charity and good deeds, all undone in a day! Defeated, the seth looked up at the sky. He felt as if instead of seeing one eclipsed sun, he could see several eclipsed suns! Everything he had done till today had been for nothing.

One of his muneems said with folded hands, "Dharamavtar, there is nothing to worry about so much. When even the ashes of a cremated body spring to life with your touch, then here we have the body itself. If dry rivers begin to gush forth once they touch your feet, wouldn't this man live again if you touch him?"

Seeing the seth's panicked face, the sethani also started to get agitated. She said, "Then why did you come here empty-handed? Do you doubt this? Go and get the pandit's body here at once."

The seth caressed the body with his hands many a time, but it would not breathe again! Now the Seth was all the more convinced that the pandit's untimely death was on his hands. *So many years of faith and charity and this is the result? How to even find out which village the pandit had come from. His family must be waiting for him . . . expecting him to return any moment.* The seth looked at the pandit. The Brahmin's eyes were wide open and the seth felt as if they asked: "You gave me the temptation of charity and called me here . . . Why did you cheat me so?"

Outside the haveli, the crowds were raising a dull roar. The seth got annoyed. "Why do you stare at my face! What can I do against God's will? Hide the body in the stores. If someone sees, there will be more *chak-chak.*"

One muneem said, "People see nothing beyond their self-interests. The people who trampled him do not even know that they trampled him. Please don't worry at all about this."

"Tomorrow at the crack of dawn, we will cremate him with sandalwood," said the sethani. "We will donate one thousand cows. His funeral procession will be carried through the streets with great pomp, and we will throw out one thousand gold mohurs! Till then, keep the body hidden in the stores."

The sethani wanted to calm the seth down. His men took the body away, but the seth kept imagining the body, still lying there. He asked the sethani, "Why did those men leave the body here?"

The sethani gave no reply. Instead she said, "It is time for you to give with your hands. Let's go downstairs."

The seth left with the sethani, but the pandit didn't leave the seth. In all four directions, the seth could only see the dead pandit's face. Troubled, the seth gave out heaps of wealth to those who had gathered.

All night, the carnival of faith and charity went on. All night, sleep eluded the seth. The sethani tried to distract her husband with chit-chat, but all the seth could see was the pandit's body. *What hopes the pandit must have come with, and what happened! All hopes . . . remained as just hopes in his heart! How will the pandit even have a good afterlife? Surely I must leave no stone unturned to organize the last rites of this man with great pomp and splendour . . . The entire realm's Brahmins will need to be fed five-five delicacies each day for a fortnight.* In these thoughts, the dark night passed.

At dawn, the seth and sethani lay thinking about the last rites that were to be performed, when all seven of the seth's muneems came in great excitement. "Dharamavtar, who compares with your generosity and good deeds! Even The Great Giver Karan[1] must be dying of shame! We had placed the pandit's body in the treasury with all the gold and pearls and locked it from outside. We just went inside and what do we see! His body has become a statue of pure gold!"

The seth stood up with a start. From his mouth escaped, "*Hain . . . Ain . . .* " But this "hain . . . ain . . . " was different from the earlier one. He half believed the accountants and half didn't believe them. He wanted to make sure with his own eyes. He quickly headed to the store.

What they had said was absolutely true! The priest's entire body had turned into a statue of pure, gleaming gold. The seth was widely recognized for his ability to tell the purity of gold. Four–five times he caressed the gold. Looking at the sethani, he said, "Pure twenty-four carat gold!"

"But what is to be so surprised about this?" his wife asked. "Are you short of gold? You must have given away scores of times more gold than this!"

Hundreds of snakes began hissing in the seth's head. He said, "You didn't quite understand what I said. If a dead body becomes a doll of pure gold by the greatness of my deeds then . . . " The seth could speak no further. The snakes began hissing louder in his head.

---

[1] Karan or Karna; a character from the Mahabharata

"Then what?" cried his wife. "I don't understand why you are so surprised at this little thing. If you ask me the truth, I think you are greater than God!"

But the seth could only hear the hissing of the snakes. Countless glistening gold dolls began dancing in front of his eyes. *There are countless people in this world, so countless golden dolls can be created!*

Stopping intermittently, the seth said, "You still haven't been able to read my mind. Countless people swarm outside like insects . . . Can't they become gold dolls like this one, locked in our stores?"

The sethani still did not understand. She said, "But how do living humans become gold dolls? The magic of your good deeds can only make *dead* bodies into gold!"

One of his clever muneems understood exactly what the seth meant. He said, "But it is the living who die! And what cause is there for these beggars to live? It would be a life well-lived if they could die and become dolls of pure gold!"

This time, the sethani could only manage, "*Hain . . . Ain . . . Ain!*"

The seth looked at his accountant. "The sethani will take a while to understand, but you have understood perfectly well what I meant. Then why do you stare at my face! In this much time, we could have made a hundred gold dolls! Go, hurry!"

All seven accountants left as soon as they got the seth's orders.'

I was also going to say 'Hain . . . Ain . . . !' like the sethani, but I pursed my lips. The spinning wheel began spinning in front of my eyes. *Ganan-ganan-ganan*!

Masi continued, 'Who can match the sorcery of this sorceress, maya. You have woven so many stories into books, but do you know any magic that is greater than that of maya? Tell me! If my sons and grandsons hadn't come under the spell of this maya, would I not have been resting and chanting God's name?'

Like the wheel she was turning, it felt like the wheel of stories was going round and round in Masi's head . . .

Translator's Note

Bijji's stories have incredible range—from legends of heroes who adventure in mythical lands full of underwater monsters, to explorers looking for untold riches; from stories about boisterous and boastful children, to tales of animal societies and families; from satire to the didactic to the absurd—there is a plethora of themes to be found. I have attempted to include a broad smattering of these different types.

In translating these stories from Rajasthani to English, I have been guided by two conservation principles. Firstly, to conserve as much of the regionality as possible. Secondly, to conserve as much of the orality as possible. These are, I feel, the two key features of the prose which must stand out starkly to a reader even when reading the translations in English.

The pursuit of these principles did present some challenges. Oral forms of stories are different from written forms, men and women speak somewhat differently, the cuss words men use are not the cuss words women use . . . These differences can often get wiped out in the act of translation. And then, of course, there is the issue of specificity of the cultural idiom—with its own rituals, sayings, cultural references, food habits, styles of speech, et cetera. The word kumbhar might be translated to potter in English, however, kumbhar denotes caste as much as occupation in Rajasthani, however in English it can end up denoting occupation only.

Moreover, Bijji was able to preserve the orality and whimsy of these stories even while setting them into written form. I have tried to preserve this lightness of form and texture by using a variety of methods—some ad hoc, some structural. These include the sprinkling of Rajasthani words throughout the prose and the use of footnotes where appropriate. I have also made liberal use of transliterated sentence structures—these sentences might appear somewhat unnatural in English; however, I felt their use to be essential to retain the texture of the originals.

I have paid particular attention to the innate quirkiness of language. For example, onomatopoeia. I've retained typical Rajasthani phrases—the words are anyway meaningless, then why translate these sounds into another language? So people still laugh dag-dag, rivers flow gal-gal and fires rage dhapal-dhapal. The use of these devices, however, stems not only as a need for workarounds to a problem, but also as a determination to challenge the reader and draw him/her into the cultural idiom of the original.

The richness and vividness of these stories comes from the granularity of these traditions—so many points of view, so many stories and so many tellings. Bijji said, 'I am less of a story writer and more of a storyteller.' And so, there are tellings and retellings. There is a freshness to be found in tapping into oral traditions that have accumulated, mutated and yet remained living over generations. It gives me great pleasure to present yet another telling of these timeless tales.

Vishes Kothari

A financial consultant by profession, Vishes Kothari has a keen interest in the oral and musical traditions of Rajasthan. He completed his masters in mathematics from the University of Cambridge, prior to which he studied at St Stephen's College, Delhi, and King's College, London. He has been associated with UNESCO-Sahapedia on projects focussed on the musical traditions of women in Rajasthan, and as a language expert with the Jaipur Virasat Foundation.

Timeless Tales from Marwar

CONTENTS

NAME: Vijaydan Detha, lovingly called Bijji

BORN: 1 September 1926 in Borunda, Rajasthan, in the Charan caste of bards and poets

FATHER: Sabaldan Detha

MOTHER: Siru Kanwar

QUALIFICATIONS: BA in Hindi from Jaswant College, Jodhpur

MARRIED TO: Sayar Kanwar

FAMOUS FOR: Vijaydan Detha is one of the most prolific and celebrated voices in India. In a career spanning decades, his writings include more than 800 short stories, many of which have been translated into multiple languages. Detha's timeless classics have been adapted into major plays and movies, some notable ones being *Paheli*, *Charandas Chor* and *Duvidha*.

MAJOR AWARDS: Padma Shri (2007), Padma Sahitya Akademi Award for Rajasthani (1974), Bhartiya Bhasa Parishad Award (1992), Marudhara Puraskar (1995), Bihari Puraskar (2002), Sahitya Chudamani Award (2006), Rao Siha Award (2011) and Rajasthan Ratna Award (2012).

DIED: 10 November 2013

ALL ABOUT DETHA

How did Vijaydan Detha's early life shape him?

Vijaydan Detha was born in 1926 in Borunda in the Marwar region of Rajasthan in the Charan caste of bards and poets. His grandfather, Jugtidan Detha, was a renowned poet in the classical Dingal tradition of poetry of Rajasthan. His father, Sabaldan Detha, was also a poet. However, unlike his ancestors, he was not interested in the verse and prose that was written to glorify forts and palaces and their inhabitants. In his works, we find voices that are not heard often. All the stories in *Batan ri Phulwari* were collected by Bijji from Borunda and its surroundings. After nightfall, when men would sit around at the village chowk, chatting and telling stories to one another, Bijji would go and join in; many a time he would contribute and tell his own stories, and at times, he would just listen. Indeed, he was surely most fascinated by the storytelling, especially stories shared by the women.

How did Bijji become a writer?

In 1959, Bijji returned to Borunda and resolved to continue writing only in Rajasthani, his mother tongue. This proved to be a turning point. Bijji formed a great intellectual partnership with the pioneering ethnomusicologist Komal Kothari. The result of this partnership was the Rupayan Sansthan. The institution did a vast amount of work on the oral and performing traditions of Rajasthan. Under the aegis of this institution, Bijji began to publish the folk tales of Rajasthan in their monthly journals, which later were compiled together and published as volumes of the *Batan ri Phulwari* collection. *Batan ri Phulwari*, literally translating to 'Garden of Tales', is a fourteen-volume collection of folk stories collected and written over nearly five decades. The literature of Rajasthan is usually thought of in the binary of *khyaat* and *baat*. Khyaat are the chronicles and praises of kings and rulers, while baat are imaginary tales that need not be historical. This collection falls into the latter category.

What were his great achievements?

Bijji was awarded the Sahitya Akademi Award for Rajasthani in 1974 for Volume 10 of this collection. Subsequently, he was also awarded the Padma Shri in 2007. In 2012, he received the highest civilian honour in the state of Rajasthan, the Rajasthan Ratna Award. Over the years, Mani Kaul (*Duvidha*, 1973), Shyam Benegal (*Charandas Chor*, 1975), Prakash Jha (*Parinati*, 1986) and Amol Palekar (*Paheli*, 2005) have adapted his works to the celluloid, while his stories have also been adapted for the theatre stage by Habib Tanvir and for television by Uday Prakash.

Oral Traditions and Folklore

It is important to understand the form and context of Vijaydan Detha's layered tales. Indeed, these tales are not as simple as they may seem on the surface; they are often critiques of powerful men, such as the landlord or the king, and about injustice, complex human relationships and nature. Since oral or verbal stories are different from written forms, they too are inscribed in a different way. Since oral or verbal stories are different from written forms, they are inscribed in a different way too. India has a rich oral storytelling tradition, where stories and folk tales are passed down from one person to the other over generations. To know more about the oral culture and writing, we look to Bijji's own words below—because what's more perfect than hearing it from the master storyteller himself!

Understanding Oral Traditions and Storytelling Culture of India

'Many problems arise when adapting the oral form of folk tales into written form. The traditional forms of the lyrics of folk songs are more or less set. There are minor variations from their traditional forms due to lapses in memory, but remembering the lyrics by heart is a key skill of the singer. But old folk tales are another matter altogether. The main thing is storyline. Thereafter, it is the storyteller's creativity, imagination, narration, intelligence and memory, which nurtures and brings out the beauty of the storyline. There are some storytellers who are so bad that they can ruin a story, while others can tell a story so beautifully that the story just must be heard. When every storyteller tells these ancient stories in their own styles, then after hearing a story, writing it as exactly as it was heard is also not enough. A command of the language alone is not enough to write a folk tale; for this, along with a command of the language, a command of the art of storytelling is of utmost importance.

When telling a story, the storyteller is in front of us and the listener and the storyteller have an attachment. When a storyteller tells a story in flesh and blood, then along with her tongue, the emotions on her face, her hands and her eyes all work together—this gives the story agility, sweetness and a life force. But in the case of written stories, the writer remains invisible. Because of this, there is no attachment between the writer and the reader. The writer must make up for the emotions on her face, her hands and her eyes through his writing alone. So knowing the language well is not enough on its own. Many other things are essential for this. A familiarity with old tales, the rituals and customs of society, history and sociology and most important, the art of writing. Broadly speaking, without these things, a written story remains flawed.

There are two straightforward ways to increase the canon of Rajasthani literature. One is to give old stories new forms and the other is to cast new stories and realities into ancient forms. Stories told through motifs of birds and animals are highly impactful on the heart. The new literature of today's new world also looks to lean on such motifs. Its new turn is to move towards such motifs.

It is also extremely important to publish the endless treasure of the Vedas, Upanishads, Puranas, Mahabharata, Ramayana, Jataka, Panchatantra, Kathasaritsagara et cetera in Rajasthani. It is only by knowing old traditions that the child of an Indian will become Indian. Else in its own country, the child will remain a foreigner. Today, we must erect a new India on the foundations of the old India. Dreams that are rootless are lies. If we don't fully know our traditions, the progress of the future will not know us.

I have collected all these stories from my village Borunda itself. Just like folk songs, this treasure of folk tales is found in endless measure with women. I did not give any story a written form without hearing it myself. I have recreated the stories' traditional forms with my art and imagination.'

—Vijaydan Detha

© Mahendra Dan Detha

SOME THINGS TO DO

Have you ever heard stories from your parents, grandparents and other older family members? You can ask your family the following questions and then trace where the stories originated from.

- Ask them where they heard these stories and at what age? Were they told these tales as bedtime stories or were there special occasions, like a religious occasion?
- Can you spot any themes in these stories? Are they related to the region that your family hails from?
- How are these stories different from the stories in the books you might have read? Do these stories remind you of some fairy tales you might have read?

If you were to write the stories that you have heard or that have been narrated to you, how different do you think the written form would be from the oral storytelling? In what ways would it be different? To know the answer, after you've documented the findings, ask your family member to recall and recite their favourite story to you.

References

Chapter 1: The Tale of Tell and Don't-Tell

1. Vijaydan Detha, 'Ke Ar Mat Ke', *Batan ri Phulwari*, Vol. 11 (Rajasthan: Rajasthani Granthagar).

Chapter 2: The Winds of Time

1. Vijaydan Detha, 'Vagat Vagat Ro Bayro', *Batan ri Phulwari*, Vol. 12 (Rajasthan: Rajasthani Granthagar).
2. Ibid., Vol. 1, second revised edition (2013).
3. This is a *choga*, meaning 'a poem'. It is based on the choga of Dari Doto, Vol. 11.

Chapter 3: Jheentiya

1. The tale of the adventures of Jheentiya is one of the most popular folk tales told to children in Rajasthan. I also heard this story as a child—a somewhat different version. It has several variations in storyline with diversions of varying lengths. However, the main storyline remains more or less the same.

2. Vijaydan Detha, 'Chal Meri Dhemki Dhamak Dham', *Batan ri Phulwari*, Vol. 2 (Rajasthan: Rajasthani Granthagar).
3. Ibid., Vol. 1 (2013).

Chapter 4: The Learning of Toil

1. Vijaydan Detha, 'Jhupdi Ro Gyan', *Batan ri Phulwari*, Vol. 5 (Rajasthan: Rajasthani Granthagar).
2. Extracted from a letter from Bijji to Malchand Tiwari, dated 24 January 2007, published in *Lok Sanskriti* journal, October 2008, trans. from Rajasthani to English by the translator.

Chapter 5: Sonal Bai

1. Vijaydan Detha, 'Sonal Bai', *Batan ri Phulwari*, Vol. 2 (Rajasthan: Rajasthani Granthagar).
2. Ibid., Vol. 8. Trans. from Hindi by the translator.

Chapter 6: Aahedi, the Hunter

1. Vijaydan Detha, 'Aahedi', *Batan ri Phulwari*, Vol. 12 (Rajasthan: Rajasthani Granthagar).
2. Komal Kothari, Ibid., first edition.

Chapter 7: Joo, Joo, Where Do You Go?

1. Vijaydan Detha, 'Joo-Joo Sidh Jave?', *Batan ri Phulwari*, Vol. 2 (Rajasthan: Rajasthani Granthagar).
2. Extracted from a letter from Bijji to Malchand Tiwari, dated 24 January 2007, published in *Lok Sanskriti* journal, October 2008, trans. from Rajasthani to English by the translator.

Chapter 8: The Joo's Curse

1. Vijaydan Detha, 'Khari Ganga Balad Khandiyo', *Batan ri Phulwari*, Vol. 2 (Rajasthan: Rajasthani Granthagar).

Chapter 9. The Farming of Pearls

1. Vijaydan Detha, 'Motyan Ri Kheti', *Batan ri Phulwari*, Vol. 12 (Rajasthan: Rajasthani Granthagar).
2. Extracted from the letter from Bijji to Malchand Tiwari, published in *Lok Sanskriti* journal, 2007.

Chapter 10: The Kelu Tree

1. Vijaydan Detha, 'Kelu Ri Kamb', *Batan ri Phulwari*, Vol. 9 (Rajasthan: Rajasthani Granthagar).
2. Ibid., first edition.

Chapter 11: Naagan, May Your Line Prosper

1. Vijaydan Detha, 'Naagan Tharo Bans Badhe', *Batan ri Phulwari*, Vol. 10 (Rajasthan: Rajasthani Granthagar).
2. Extracted from a letter from Mani Kaul to Bijji, dated 21 May 1972. Published in ibid., 2008 reprint edition.
3. The choga has been taken from Naharsingh Bachrajsingh, Vol. 9.

Chapter 12: Eternal Hope

1. Vijaydan Detha, 'Aasa Amardhan', *Batan ri Phulwari*, Vol. 4 (Rajasthan: Rajasthani Granthagar).

2.   Extracted from a letter from Bijji to Malchand Tiwari, dated 24 January 2007, published in *Lok Sanskriti* journal, October 2008, trans. from Rajasthani to English by the translator.

Chapter 13: The Thakar's Ghost

1.   Vijaydan Detha, 'Thakar Ro Bhoot', *Batan ri Phulwari*, Vol. 9 (Rajasthan: Rajasthani Granthagar).
2.   As mentioned in ibid., first edition of Vol. 9.
3.   Extracted from a letter from Bijji to Malchand Tiwari, dated 24 January 2007. Published in *Lok Sanskriti* journal, October 2008.

Chapter 14: The Gulgula Tree

1.   Vijaydan Detha, 'Gulgula Ro Gaach', *Batan ri Phulwari*, Vol. 9 (Rajasthan: Rajasthani Granthagar).
2.   Ibid., first edition.

Chapter 15: To Each His Own

1.   Vijaydan Detha, 'Nyara Nyara Sukh', *Batan ri Phulwari*, Vol. 4 (Rajasthan: Rajasthani Granthagar).
2.   Extracted from a letter from Bijji to Mahasweta Devi, dated 28 March 2002.

Chapter 16: The Leaf and the Pebble

1.   Vijaydan Detha, 'Paan Ar Dhaglo', *Batan ri Phulwari*, Vol. 2 (Rajasthan: Rajasthani Granthagar).
2.   Detha to Malchand Tiwari, published in *Lok Sanskriti*, 2007.

Chapter 17: Jaraav Masi's Tales

1. Vijaydan Detha, 'Lichmi Ra Chala', 'Aa Maya Kamangari', *Batan ri Phulwari*, Vol. 5 (Rajasthan: Rajasthani Granthagar).
2. Detha in an interview with *The Hindu*, published 9 September 2013.

The India Pages

1. Detha, *Batan ri Phulwari*, Vol. 2, first edition (1963).